DEATH IN THE DARK

Leon lay rigid under his blanket with his eyes wide open.

Someone was creeping around in the night not so very far away. He cocked his head to the side and listened more closely. Two of them.

Dumb bastards, he thought. He had been snuck up on by Apaches and Kiowas and Comanches and those fellows were a whole lot better at it than these ones were.

Leon smiled silently toward the stars, and snaked his hand out from under the blanket to reach his holstered Army Colt.

These two bushwhackers were in for a surprise. They wouldn't be the first—and Leon could be grimly sure they wouldn't be the last. . . .

THE OUTSIDER

Frank Roderus

A SIGNET BOOK

NEW AMERICAN LIBRARY

SIGNET, SIGNET CLASSIC, MENTOR, ONYX, PLUME, MERIDIAN and NAL BOOKS are published by NAL PENGUIN INC., 1633 Broadway, New York, New York 10019

First Printing, October, 1988

1 2 3 4 5 6 7 8 9

PRINTED IN THE UNITED STATES OF AMERICA

For Bob and Jane Phillips

1

The big Studebaker rocked from side to side, bouncing wildly on its leather suspension as first the front wheel and then the rear jolted over a slab of rock that intruded into the roadbed. Leon grabbed the metal railing and clung to it, not at all sure the stagecoach driver would stop for him if he fell off his precarious perch on the roof of the coach.

He slipped toward the edge, caught himself, and pushed back into the middle where he could brace against a steamer trunk that was lashed to the roof rack. The trunk was too large to fit into the luggage boot attached to the back of the big Studebaker.

The coach could carry a dozen passengers inside its roomy interior, and there was provision for extra seats to be bolted onto the roof where Leon now rode.

At the moment, though, there were only seven passengers riding inside the Studebaker. And no extra seat had been fitted to the roof.

The coach lurched again. Leon grabbed a guy rope that crisscrossed the top of the trunk, and pressed the sole of his boot against the railing to jam himself in place while the driver snapped his whip in the air behind the ears of the off leader and spoke to his team.

"Hyup. Hyup now. Pull it."

The Studebaker dropped into the bottom of a sandy wash that crossed the road, slowed slightly as it climbed out on the other side, and settled into a reasonably smooth roll again as the rutted road stretched flat and empty before them.

Leon peeked past the driver's shoulder to make sure

there were no more obstructions ahead, then released his
grip on the rope long enough to pull his battered old
campaign hat off and wipe his forehead with the back of
his wrist.

Arizona was as hot as west Texas and New Mexico
had been. The sun was a fierce, palpable weight on his
shoulders. It baked through the wool of his shirt and
burned into the back of his neck through the kerchief he
wore there, from long experience and painful early les-
sons, to protect himself from sunburn. The heat from the
sun made even the cloth of his trousers hot to the touch
when he laid his hand on his thigh and gulped for breath,
yearning now for the clean, sweet air of winter. But winter was a long time past in this country. It was springtime
now.

If this was spring in Arizona, what in hell was summer
going to be like?

He probably had it right the first time, Leon reflected.
Hell was just what it was going to be. He smiled a little
to himself. That was going to be all right too.

Leon had already been to hell. He had earned his way
out of it too, and from now on he would be working for
himself.

He broke into a broad, gap-toothed grin at that thought:
no more reveille bugles at five-thirty in the morning; no
more yessir and nossir; no more useless, make-work labor details; no more going out in search of trouble.

His grin got wider.

The next cold, wet saddle he crawled onto before day-
break would be his cold, wet saddle, by damn. The next
stable he cleaned out would be his own stable.

Even now, even so close and closer with every turn of
the Studebaker's wheels, he could hardly believe it.

Yet the deed to the land lay right this very moment,
folded and oilskin-wrapped and more precious than gold
or diamonds, inside the money belt at his waist. A deed
to actual land, written out and duly recorded in the Comas County courthouse.

A deed to his land.

Lordy, but that was something.

The big coach swayed and bumped on into the morning. Off in the distance there still wasn't any sign of a town, but Kazumal had to be close now. Leon hadn't wanted to ask anyone, but he had overheard one of the passengers talking with the driver at the last stop. Kazumal was supposed to be the next relay point, and this team had been pulling hard for better than two hours now. It had to be near.

He began to sit straighter, his brown eyes fixed toward the horizon, waiting for that first look at the place that was going to be his home for the rest of his days.

He found himself becoming tense and—he admitted it to himself—excited too.

If he had been alone—say, just himself and a horse out on this flat, hot road—Leon would have burst out with one of the old spirituals he remembered his grandmother singing when she was happy. Because Lord knew, Leon Brown had never had a happier moment in his whole life than this one that was coming up at the next stage stop.

Instead he forced himself to keep his big mouth shut and his trembling under control.

The near wheeler threw its head and rolled its eyes as a small bird fluttered into unexpected flight beside its head. The driver cursed, unmindful of the ears of the lady who rode in the coach beneath his box, and pulled the stout horse back into line with a cruel jerk on the animal's bit.

Let 'em run, Leon found himself silently urging. Let 'em take it at a gallop the whole rest of the way there.

He was grinning again now, and no matter how hard he tried to control it, he could not make himself quit.

Next stop Kazumal.

Next stop home.

2

"Boy!"

Leon tensed, but he kept his face impassive. Nothing, not even this driver, was going to spoil it for him now.

At the thought of how wonderful this day was, he very nearly responded, in fact, with another broad grin.

"Boy, you untie that trunk there and hand it down to me. And mind you do it gentle. Don't be throwing it around. Hand it down gentle."

Leon nodded and began to untie the steamer trunk that had been his traveling companion on the roof of the Studebaker for the past five days, ever since he reached this section of the line and started the last, westward leg toward Kazumal.

He untied the cords and coiled them as neatly as he would have fashioned a picket rope, then lifted the trunk—the thing was big and awkward and incredibly heavy—and eased it over the side of the coach and down to where the driver and a helper from the depot could take it from him.

The two men accepted the trunk and carried it toward the depot without so much as a grunt by way of a thank you. Leon had not expected anything different, and the oversight in manners bothered him not at all.

The gentlemen passengers who had ridden inside the coach were already out and on their way, but the lady who had been among them was still inside the Studebaker fixing or fussing or whatever it was ladies did. Leon could feel the body of the big coach shift as she moved about.

He waited patiently where he was until she finally disembarked from the coach, a nicely dressed gentleman rushing to help her down the steps, then Leon swung a leg over the side of the roof and climbed down over the luggage boot.

He planted his boots wide on the dusty, sunbaked soil of Kazumal and this time he was unable to keep from breaking into a huge smile.

"What the hell are you hanging around for, boy?" The driver and the depot helper were on the boardwalk now, staring—glaring was more like it—at him.

"Just getting my things."

The driver grunted. "Make sure that's all you take. I'm watching you."

Leon knew good and well what was expected. The coach driver wanted him to tug his forelock and bob his head and maybe do a little foot shuffle in the street while he said "Yessir" and "Nossir I won't, sir" and all that old line.

Well, the son of a bitch could wait until Kazumal froze over in the middle of August if he expected that now.

Leon Brown was done saying "sir" to any man.

Leon picked up the big, lumpy canvas sack that was his luggage and the pair of much-patched saddlebags and carried them off down the street.

There was no point in asking either of those fellows back at the depot where Lawyer Farr's office was.

No need for it either. Kazumal was not so big that he wouldn't be able to find it with a little looking.

Somehow Leon had expected Kazumal to be a little bigger than it was. Not that he was complaining. He was sure the town was just right.

Up at this end where the Dickinson and Haines Express Company had its offices there were four, five blocks of businesses. Scattered around on both sides of the main street were some smaller streets and avenues that had houses lining them. Down at the other end of town he could see a second business and residential section mixed together, the buildings at that end of town made of adobe in the Mexican style he had seen back in Texas. That end of town was dominated by the crumbling adobe bell tower of an old church.

This end was where Lawyer Farr's office would likely be.

He walked past a two-story building with a false-front third floor that was the town's hotel, two stores advertising general merchandise, and a butcher shop and a café the smells coming out of the café made his saliva flow; it had been quite a while since a poor breakfast—and on into the next block.

Another false-front building was City Hall, with a small addition at the side that had a sign reading TOWN MARSHAL.

The place Leon wanted was in the next block. A small sign was posted next to an outside stairway leading to a second-story set of offices. The sign read J. WALTER FARR, *Attorney at Law, Land Agent, Notary Public.*

Leon was trembling as he mounted the wooden steps.

The door to Lawyer Farr's office stood open, as were the few windows. There was no breeze to cut the heat of the early afternoon.

Leon stepped inside without knocking, set his bag down, and removed his hat. The inside of Farr's office was hot, but at least the shade of being indoors lent an illusion of coolness.

"Mr. Farr?"

A man in shirt sleeves seated behind a cluttered desk looked up with sudden alarm that moderated quickly to mere suspicion when Leon continued to stand with his hat in one hand and the saddlebags in the other.

"Who are you? What do you want here?"

"I came to pick up my key, Mr. Farr. Your letter said—"

"My letter? What letter? I've never written you any letter."

"You are Lawyer Farr, aren't you?"

"Yes, what of it? I've never written you any letter."

Leon chuckled. The misunderstanding was normal enough, of course, and innocent too. All their past business had been conducted through the mails while Leon was waiting for his enlistment to expire. The lawyer simply hadn't known.

Leon had to admit that it was probably quite a start for the man to look up now and see someone like Leon standing in front of him wanting his key. And of course there wasn't any denying that this pale, pudgy, sweat-soaked fellow might feel a trifle intimidated when he got a first look at his recent client.

Leon was well over six feet tall and was built with the muscle and vitality of a blooded stallion at its prime. He had always been tall, but back when he first enlisted, he had been thin and gangly. If the army had known how he would fill out his bones, they never would have accepted him into the cavalry, and he would have spent his whole time walking in the dust with the mudball infantry.

Leon was not particularly prosperous-looking in the remnants of what had once been a uniform. His much-washed blue trousers still showed dark-blue stripes down the legs where he had removed the yellow cavalry stripes from them.

The biggest shock for Farr, though, would be the fact that Leon's skin was a deep, rich, satiny brown.

He wasn't black. Exactly. Not so dark as some of the men in the Tenth had been. And he wasn't any coffee-with-cream mulatto either. What he was, he thought, was just about right. A healthy, vibrant cocoa shade with just a hint of copper undertone.

"I am Leon Brown, Mr. Farr," Leon explained. "I bought the old Harrold place from you. I have the papers right here—"

"You can't be," Farr blurted.

"But—"

"You're a nigger," the lawyer added.

Only the slightest flicker in Leon's eyes betrayed his reaction. He nodded. "So I am, Mr. Farr. I have been all my life. It wasn't a recent decision."

"But—"

This time it was Leon who interrupted. "I will thank you for the key you've been holding for me, Mr. Farr, and for directions to my property."

"What the hell are the people of this town going to

think when they learn I've gone and sold land to a nigger?" Farr complained.

"I wouldn't know about that, Mr. Farr. What I was hoping when I chose to locate here was that folks who have problems like Apaches to worry about weren't going to be so fretful about race when another homesteader comes among them who can stand up and help when the time comes."

Farr was not listening. He was much too deep into his own worries to be paying attention to anything that Leon Brown might wish to say.

"You can't . . . you can't have that property, boy. I'm sorry, but there's been a misunderstanding . . ."

The politeness went out of Leon's expression. His dark eyes hardened, and he held himself stiffly erect in the doorway of J. Walter Farr, Attorney at Law, et cetera. "I have the deed in my pocket, Mr. Farr. You know my title is valid. You filed it yourself. The chaplain back at Fort Larned looked it over for me. I own that land, Mr. Farr. Own it free and clear and beholden to no man. Now are you going to give me my key"—Leon paused for a moment, then smiled—"or am I going to go out on the streets of this town and tell all the good folks here what a nice, helpful man their Lawyer Farr is and how much he did for me so I could come here and live?"

Farr's face and neck flushed a bright, florid red. "You wouldn't . . . you wouldn't do that."

Leon grinned at him.

"Would you?"

The grin became wider.

Farr snatched a drawer open, angrily pulled out a small envelope, and slapped it down hard on the desktop. "Take it. Take it and get out of here. And don't come back."

"Directions to the place, Mr. Farr?"

"There's a map. In with the key. Now get out of my office."

"Thank you kindly, Mr. Farr."

Leon picked up the envelope and slipped it inside his

shirt close to the money belt where his deed and the rest of his savings were. "Thank you very much."

He picked up his bag, dragged the old campaign hat over his close-cropped scalp—a popular hairstyle among the men of the Tenth, if only because it frustrated the hell out of Indians looking for lodge decorations—and went back out into the glaring sunshine of Kazumal's main street.

3

There was no back door to either of Kazumal's restaurants and therefore no place where Leon might have gone to buy a meal. Even at the army posts where he had served for three enlistments, even after he wore a corporal's proud stripes on his sleeve, there had never been a civilian restaurant where a Negro trooper could walk inside and sit down to a meal. He knew better than to expect any different in Kazumal, and he had no intention of subjecting himself to the rejection that would follow if he tried to enter a public café.

He settled for going into one of the general mercantiles and buying a meal off the grocery shelves. White diners would not consider sitting next to a black man in a restaurant, but Leon had never yet known a white storekeeper who would refuse his money when he wanted to shop in their stores.

He carried cheese and crackers and a can of peaches that tasted faintly of tin outside and found a patch of shade in a back alley where he could eat in solitary comfort.

While he ate he examined the map Lawyer Farr had given him. The map was crudely drawn but seemed simple enough. All he had to do was follow the public road south six miles, turn off at the Harrold marker, and go another five miles.

Leon felt a catch in his chest as he realized that for much of the time after leaving the public road he would already be traveling on his own deeded property.

Lordy, but knowing that made him feel good.

Twenty-seven sections of land. Twenty-seven square

miles of it. Seventeen thousand two hundred eighty acres of his ground, purchased at just over twelve cents an acre.

He found himself smiling as he squatted in the shade of the alley.

Fifteen years of scrimping every penny. Fifteen years of six-for-five loans to the profligate enlisted men of the Tenth.

His smile stretched into a grin. This result would have been worth twice the time and two times twice the effort.

Leon finished the peaches and carefully rewrapped what was left of the cheese and hard crackers. There probably wouldn't be any supplies left in the ranch house. Farr's letters had said the place was sitting empty for a time. First he would have to buy a horse, of course. The place was supposed to be stocked, but the horses would be scattered. They couldn't have been left corralled with no one there to care for them. He sighed, happily contemplating all the things that were to come. He would have to buy some groceries to take out to the place with him. He would have to. . . .

He would have to quit lazing in the shade, that was what he would have to do.

He stuffed the crackers and cheese into his saddlebags and stood, suddenly eager to complete the business he had to tend to here in Kazumal and get out to his house. To his home.

There was going to be a lot of work to do. He knew that. And he wanted everything to be perfect when Anne May arrived.

He wanted to get started.

Most of all he wanted to see it for himself.

Still smiling, he picked up his things and hurried toward the livery he had seen near the express-company office.

The livery man barely bothered to turn his head aside before he spat, the stream of yellow-brown juice raising a puff of dust where it landed close to Leon's left boot.

"Take it or leave it. That's the only horse I got to sell, and that's the only price I'll take for it."

Leon eyed the animal in question with undisguised skepticism.

The livery man claimed the seal-brown horse was nine years old. A look at the brown's teeth, though, showed double that age. Leon said nothing about the discrepancy.

"At that price," he said, "you throw in a saddle, bridle, blanket, and bit, right?"

Even at that the man was asking several times what a good horse would have been worth. This brown had not been a good horse ten years ago, and age had improved it not a whit.

"At that price you get the horse. You want more, buy more. I got some stuff here I might sell you." The man smirked and spat again. "If the price's right."

The man was trying to rob him, plain and simple. Horse and saddle at this rate would take most of what Leon had left from his savings. He couldn't do it. It wouldn't be fair to Anne May and their hopes for the future. It would be particularly foolish when there were horses of his own and cattle of his own carrying W. T. Harrold's—carrying Leon's—3H brand right out at the place.

"I'm sorry. I just can't do that."

The man looked smug and unconcerned. "You do whatever you want, nigger. Doesn't matter to me."

Leon didn't react to the taunt. He thanked the man and picked up his bags.

It was going to be a long walk out to the 3H Ranch.

4

It was nearly dark by the time Leon reached the 3H. For
the past hour and a half he had been walking across his
own land. The fact was exhilarating. But not enough so
to keep his feet from hurting. Fifteen years on the back
of a cavalry horse had not prepared him for an eleven-
mile walk.

He stopped a quarter-mile out from the 3H ranch house
and looked out through the twilight.

This was the most beautiful thing he had ever seen.

The house was low and small, a single story built of
stone and adobe with a sod roof spread over stout poles.
The door was centered in the front wall, and there were
window openings on either side of it. Anne May would
be able to look out over their land while she was inside
doing her work.

A stone-walled well was dug to the left of the house,
and a copse of old, gnarled cottonwoods grew behind it,
hinting at a pond or seep to be found there.

Beyond the well to the south were the remains of the
corrals. The uprights still stood, but there were few rails
left. Most of the rails had either fallen down or been
taken for firewood by passersby. A shed built of mud and
wattle was behind the corrals, its roof sagging and badly
in need of fresh sod to turn the rain.

There were no barns, no bunkhouse, no windmill, and
no sign of life of any kind.

All in all, Leon found it lovely beyond description.

He hefted his canvas duffel onto his shoulder and
walked the last little way to the house.

As he came closer, he smiled ruefully, thinking of the

key in his shirt, the key Lawyer Farr had been so reluctant to give him.

The door to the house stood open, hanging drunkenly from a single leather hinge, and the window shutters were open wide as well.

"Good thing I don't know anybody that I want to keep out," he said to himself.

He paused outside the door for a moment and ran his palm almost reverently over the dry, aging wood of the doorframe.

"Leon Brown has come home," he declared in a loud, firm voice. And stepped inside.

Leon walked back to Kazumal two days later. He hated having to leave the place when there was yet so much work to be done, but he had no choice. He had forgotten to buy food before he started out his first day home, and his belly gnawed and rumbled emptily now that the last of the cheese and crackers was gone. Besides, he needed to buy tools—the place had not been nearly so well equipped as Lawyer Farr had led him to believe by mail— and he wanted to post the letter to Anne May telling her about the home that awaited her arrival.

The walk took just under four hours, but he started well before daylight and was on the city streets before the town's small bank opened for business.

Leon intended to do no banking, though, so that didn't matter. Most of his savings lay buried in the ground beside the well wall. Banks could fail. Chaplain Gleason of the Tenth had taught him that long ago when the chaplain was busy teaching all of the recruits to read and to cipher and to learn all the other new and wonderful things that life was opening to them. Leon had never trusted a bank in his life and didn't intend to start doing so now. The little he thought he would need for his shopping was in his pocket.

He went to the same mercantile where he had done business before. A woman was coming out onto the boardwalk. Leon removed his hat and stepped quickly down onto the street, averting his eyes from her as she passed. The woman went by without seeming to notice him standing there, although every man Leon had passed in Kazumal had been open enough in their stares.

No one here was accustomed to seeing a man of color on their streets, he realized. He didn't worry about that. They would grow used to it soon enough.

He waited in the street until the lady was well down the block, then went inside the store. The proprietor gave him a noncommittal look but no greeting.

"I need to buy some food," Leon told him. "And I'd like to look at your tools."

"Do you have a list of what you want?"

"I do." Leon handed it over. The list was short enough, but then Leon's needs were few. A tin of lard. Cornmeal. Salt. Sugar. Oatmeal. He loved his coffee, a taste acquired and through the years nurtured while he was in the army, but he would forgo that pleasure until he could find his cattle and perhaps sell some of the culls. Coffee was too expensive, the other needs too great—at least for the time being. Water would do for now.

And one thing he definitely would not, not ever, buy would be beans.

Lordy, but he had come to despise the beans and the rancid bacon that was the usual fare in the Tenth. He hoped he never had to eat either of those victuals again.

"This won't take me but a minute to fill," the store-keeper said. "The tools are over there."

Leon thanked the man and found a haphazard display of tools in the corner indicated. He selected an ax, a bucksaw—one saw would have to do for his wood cutting and finish work too—and a small reel of wire that he could use for repairing the corrals. Hammer and nails would have been better, but he doubted that he could afford or, for that matter, carry much in the way of bought nails.

By the time he was done shopping, the proprietor had his food order on the counter.

Leon bundled it all into the empty duffel he had brought with him, and paid for his purchases.

"Thank you."

The man grunted and turned away. He had seemed at least a little friendlier than that just a few minutes earlier. Now he was sour again. Leon saw the reason for the change when he shouldered his bag and turned toward the door. Leon was no longer the only customer in the place.

Two young men, the younger of them scarcely more than a boy, stood there staring at him.

Despite their age, both wore revolvers on their belts. But then, that did seem to be the custom of this country. Most of the men Leon saw on the streets were armed. They probably had good reason for that, he realized. He should have thought to bring his army .45 today. There was still plenty of threat from raiding Apaches here. He probably was foolish to have left home unarmed himself.

He started toward the door, but neither of the newcomers moved aside. They were standing just inside and were blocking his exit. Or perhaps waiting to see if he would push through them.

Leon didn't want trouble. Not with these boys or with anyone else. He stepped out of the aisle between the store counters and waited, pretending to examine a display of bolting cloth piled there.

"See, Tom? He's more yella than black."

The other one chuckled.

Leon did not look to see which of them was trying to impress the other. It didn't matter.

"Isn't that right, nigger?"

Leon stiffened, but he kept his expression calm as he turned to look at the two of them. "Were you speaking to me?"

"You see any other niggers around here, boy?" It was the older one who was doing the pushing. The younger seemed to be enjoying the show.

Both boys were blond, with the same shade of lank hair and thin faces and prominent noses. Leon suspected the two were brothers.

"No, I don't," Leon said calmly.

It wasn't what he wanted to do. He wanted to ignore them. No, the truth was he wanted to teach them the same lesson a good many snooty, snotty white troopers had been given behind the cavalry stables. But that would be a mistake.

"You know your place, boy?" the older brother asked.

Leon smiled. "Oh, yes. I would say that I do." The slabs of thick muscle across his shoulders corded and his fists knotted, but he kept all of that out of his expression and continued to smile pleasantly at the ignorant boy.

Ignorant, that was what Chaplain Gleason explained such people were. Ignorant trash. They could come in any color, including Leon's, as had been demonstrated by some of the troopers in his own outfit.

"Do not confuse ignorance with stupidity," the chaplain had told them. "Stupidity is something a person can't help. A stupid man is to be pitied. But ignorance is a sin. Ignorance is the blind, willful refusal to learn. That is a sin, and it is to be despised. Remember that. Pity the stupid and avoid the ignorant, and your lives will be easier."

These boys were ignorant.

"Good," the first youngster said. "Now step outa our way."

Leon was already well out of the center of the aisle. He looked at the boy and decided maybe he was stupid as well as ignorant and therefore deserving of more pity than contempt. Amusement tugged at Leon's lips as he backed the rest of the way against the counter where the cloth was displayed. He could break either or both of these boys without having to think twice about it, and yet they stood there believing they were getting the better of him. When he thought about it, it was more laughable than aggravating.

The younger one grinned and the two of them marched grandly down the aisle past Leon.

"Yella is as yella does," the younger one muttered as he went by.

Leon shook his head and went back out into the glare of the morning sunshine.

5

Except for the fact that he couldn't find any of the live-stock that were supposed to be on the place, things were coming along well now.

He had salvaged all the old rails he could and cut some new ones on the hill behind the house—cedar or piñon or perhaps juniper, Leon didn't know which was which and didn't particularly care—and carried them laboriously down a few at a time until the smaller corral was completely rebuilt. The big pen would have to wait, but there would be no need for it anyway until he found his cattle.

The inside of the house was as comfortable as he could make it. He had replastered the chimney with fresh mud and scoured the cast-iron stove with sand, water, and elbow grease until there was not a trace of rust or soot on it. It would be nice if he could afford some stove blacking before Anne May arrived, but he would have to wait and see about that. It would partially depend on when she got here, and he still had no idea when that would be. It might be weeks yet before her answer reached him through the mail.

He had no ladder, but he had fashioned a step stool of sorts out of an old crate he found in the trash dump Harrold had left near the small, muddy pond. The trash dump had become practically a market for Leon, supplying him with all manner of odds and ends that he found useful.

Empty cans, washed with the crushed roots of the yucca, known in the cavalry as "soapweed," and scrubbed with sand, became cups and bowls and baking tins, since there was no tableware in the house. More cans flattened and chopped to shape became spoons and crude forks. Still other cans crushed, twisted, and bent to form became hardware to secure the rehung door and shutters.

Leon was genuinely pleased that W. T. Harrold had been a man who liked to eat canned foods.

Now Leon was busy trying to rebuild the roof of the shed. Not that he had anything to store inside the shed, exactly, but if the structure was going to be on his property, it should be tight and tidy.

He was busy laying fresh sod over the new roof poles when he heard the approach of a horse. He stopped his work and looked out across the dry, arid expanse of range toward the rider.

He didn't recognize the man, but then he wouldn't have expected to. The horse was small and short-coupled, at least a full hand shorter than the leggy cavalry horses Leon was used to. It moved nicely, though, he thought. Light and shifty on its small feet. Its rider was sunburned and dusty from travel, a tall, gray-haired man with a sweep of mustache almost as wide as his head. He crossed the earth yard to the shed and stopped there looking up at Leon on the roof.

"You're welcome to water for yourself and your horse, mister," Leon said. "And I have some corn cakes left over. They're cold, but you're welcome to them."

The visitor continued to stare at him for a moment, then nodded and dismounted. He led his horse to the well and drew a bucket of water, which he poured into the hollowed log trough Leon had dragged there. While the horse drank, the man walked over to the newly repaired corral and appeared to be studying the gate Leon had hung. Or the ground under it.

"Is there something I can do for you, mister?"

The man turned with a grimace. For a moment he glared at Leon. Then his expression softened. "It wasn't you," he said.

"Pardon?"

"I said it wasn't you."

"Am I supposed to be glad about that or sorry?" Leon

climbed down off the roof and walked toward his odd guest.

The man cocked his head and squinted. "You aren't what I expected," he said.

Leon held his hands out in front of him and turned them as if examining their palms and backs and palms again. "A man sure gets sunburned working on a roof, doesn't he? My, oh, my, what you must think of me looking like this."

The man's lips twisted into a hint of a smile. Then he gave up trying to restrain it and let himself laugh.

"They told me about you. I wasn't sure if I should believe it or not."

"Oh, it's true, I'm afraid." Leon smiled at him.

"It was also suggested that you might be the reason I'm missing six head of beef cattle."

"I'm afraid I can't help you there. I can't find my own, much less anybody else's."

"Huh. You aren't likely to neither. Not afoot, you aren't. You don't have a horse anyplace?"

Leon shook his head. "Couldn't afford what that fellow in town was asking for his, and I can't find one of my own."

The visitor pursed his lips and twisted the right tip of his mustache. "That's what I kinda figured. There hasn't been a horse around here since the last rain, and Lord knows how long that's been. Longer'n I want to try to work out, that's for sure. Which is why I say it wasn't you that made free with my cows. I found tracks that say somebody helped 'em leave my property. Lost the tracks down on the lower part of your place. I, uh, came here thinking to accuse you."

"If you lost the tracks on my place, then I guess I can't blame you. No harm was done."

The man cocked his head to the side again. "You talk funny, you know that?"

"I do?"

"Yeah. I mean, not funny exactly. But not like a ni—uh, a Negro. I mean, you talk the same as anybody else."

"And that's funny?"

"Yeah. Yeah, it is."

"You mean I ought to say 'yowzuh' and 'bawze' and stuff like that?"

The visitor at least had the good grace to flush a pale shade of red. "Uh, something like that, yes."

Leon laughed. "Would it make you feel more comfortable if I put some mush and 'lasses in my speech?"

The red in the man's face was not so pale now. Leon thought it was glowing pretty good.

He laughed again. "Actually I did talk like that. Used to. We had a chaplain in the Tenth who taught me to speak nearly as well as a white man."

The visitor grinned. "I'm putting my foot in it pretty deep, aren't I?"

"Not so bad, really. You doin' awright for a offay."

"What?"

"Never mind."

"You said something about the Tenth? Like, what do they call them, buffalo soldiers?"

"That's right. Three hitches. I came out a corporal." Leon was unable to keep the note of pride out of his voice.

His visitor looked away into the distance. "I used to live in Texas. A bunch of buffalo soldiers from the Ninth saved my family from the Comanche once."

"I'm glad to hear that, mister."

The man turned his head so Leon couldn't see his expression and added, "They weren't around in New Mexico, though. Apache over there. I was in town that day. They were all dead when I got home that night."

"Oh." Leon examined the toe of his boot. "I'm . . . sorry." It was lame, but there wasn't much else a man could say to something like that.

"Yeah." The visitor cleared his throat. "Well. Those troopers gave me three and a half years that I wouldn't have had with them. There's that, I guess."

"Yeah, there is that. Look, uh, do you want some corn cakes or . . . ?"

"No. No, I want to get home now. My place is east

of here about ten miles. It's the next turnoff below your road.''

Leon nodded.

''The name is Ramsey. Jud Ramsey.''

''Pleased to make your acquaintance, Mr. Ramsey. I'm Leon Brown.''

''Yeah, well . . .''

''I'll try not to steal any of your cattle, Mr. Ramsey.''

A faint smile flickered on Ramsey's lips. ''I'll keep that in mind, Mr. Brown.'' He returned to his horse and stepped into the saddle.

He acted like he was going to rein away, then paused. ''Mr. Brown . . .''

''Yes?''

''You said something about finding your horses?''

''That's right. Horses and cattle too. The place is supposed to be stocked, but—''

''There aren't any horses, Mr. Brown. I knew Walt Harrold. He only owned three head of horses, and they were sold off by the estate before this place was put up for sale.''

Leon felt a bleak emptiness settle into the pit of his stomach. ''No horses?''

''Not a one. I'm sure of it. But if it makes you feel any better, there should be sixty, seventy head of cattle wearing old Walt's brand. Your brand, I guess I should say now. I haven't seen any of them lately, but then I haven't been looking either.''

''I thought—''

''You thought wrong.'' Ramsey smiled again. ''Another thing that might make you feel better, though, is to remember that that lying SOB Farr—he handled the estate for the relatives, you know—he didn't cheat you because you're a Negro. The way I hear it, Mr. Brown, he damn sure thought you were a white man when he cheated you. It's almost like you got the last laugh on him by turning up black.''

''You certainly know how to make a man feel better, Mr. Ramsey.''

Ramsey smiled. ''Good day, Mr. Brown.''

"Good day, Mr. Ramsey."

Leon's neighbor wheeled his horse away from the trough and set out toward the east.

"Son of a bitch," Leon complained aloud.

What was he going to do now? Buy that ancient nag in town, he supposed. It seemed that he was going to have little choice about it.

6

It might have been all right if the two loafers hadn't been there, leaning against the corral with elbows on the top rails, their boots propped on the bottom rails and big grins on their faces as they admired the way their pal at the livery put the nigger in his place. The livery owner in turn was posturing for his buddies, very much aware that they were behind him listening to what he was saying. The fact that Leon understood the situation didn't make it any more palatable.

"Take it or leave it," the livery man was saying with a smirk on his face, his grinning buddies behind him. "Been a lot o' interest in that horse since you was here last, y' see. Got several people wantin' to buy th' animal." The man placed a slight emphasis on the word "people," as if to imply that a black man like Leon should not be considered a person but these other prospects should. "So that's why the price's gone up."

Horse, saddle, blanket, bit, bridle . . . If Leon let this smug son of a bitch have his fun—and take his exaggerated profit—it would wipe out nearly all of his savings. There would be nothing left for him and Anne May to live on until the place was producing an income.

Leon felt like removing the smug expression from the livery man's unpleasant face. It would be so easy to do. Wipe him up and both his shit-eating friends too, damn them.

He sighed. Sure. It would be easy. And then he could spend the next six months or maybe a year sitting in a jail cell right here in Kazumal. Wouldn't that be nice for Anne May to come home to.

"Thank you for your trouble," he said politely. "I'll let you know."

"You do that." The man cackled and turned to look at his pals, probably giving them a broad wink over his shoulder, although Leon couldn't see. "O' course the price could go up again. You jus' never know." That brought a laugh from his two friends.

Leon turned and walked away.

There was no point in trying to argue with a situation like this one. And he was damn sure not going to beg that man for simple fairness.

He trudged sore-footed and suddenly weary through town.

A smile tugged at his lips while he walked. This walking to town and back was sure going to keep him from getting fat and lazy now that he was a civilian again.

Since he was in town anyway, there were a few things he might as well tend to before he started back. He had left his duffel at home and brought the saddlebags draped over his shoulder instead, thinking that he would be riding home this evening instead of walking. There was enough carrying capacity in the saddlebags, though, that he could pick up a few things he needed. And he needed to find a preacher to perform the wedding ceremony once Anne May arrived.

He stopped first at the post office, which was a caged-off area in the back of one of the stores. "Any mail for—"

"Brown, right?"

"Yes. Leon Brown. General-delivery address is what I gave."

"Nothing for you, Leon."

"You're sure?"

The mail clerk turned to check the big general-delivery pigeonhole.

The clerk already knew him by name, Leon reflected. That was interesting if not particularly surprising. And the man called him by name. Called him by his first name, of course. Leon doubted that the clerk would have been so immediately familiar with a newcome white res-

ident. Still, being called by his given name was a step up
from being called boy or nigger.

"Nope. Nothing," the clerk assured him.

Leon was disappointed. Of course it was much too
early for him to expect Anne May's answer. He knew
that. But he couldn't help being disappointed anyway.
"Thanks."

"The mail arrives three times a week," the clerk said
as Leon was turning to leave.

Leon turned back and smiled. "Thank you very
much."

"Sure. No problem."

Not everyone in Kazumal was going to be impossible
to get along with, Leon decided as he left the store. That
was something he was going to want to keep in mind in
the future as a protection against the slurs and the insults
of the ignorant ones.

He walked back out into the late-afternoon sunshine.
Lordy, but it was hot in this country. Leon's new neighbors undoubtedly were sure that a black man didn't feel
the heat and couldn't sunburn. Leon wished they were
right about that. He wiped the film of sweat off his forehead and stood on the boardwalk wondering where he
might find a preacher.

If there was a regular church in Kazumal he hadn't
seen it yet, except for the crumbling old mission down at
the other end of town. A civil marriage could probably
be performed at City Hall, but he wanted to give Anne
May something better than that to remember when they
were old.

He ambled around town a little, trying to spot a steeple
or bell tower, but apparently if the white folks of Kazumal held Sunday services, they did it without benefit
of a regular sanctuary.

He tried asking a man who was idling on a street corner, but the fellow only gave him a cussing.

"Thanks for your help." The man seemed completely
unaware of the sarcasm in Leon's voice and continued to
cuss him on down the block.

Leon gave up and went down to the Mexican end of town.

The church there didn't look like much, but the massive front doors were standing open and there were people coming and going.

Leon mounted the church steps, wiped his feet carefully, and removed his hat before he went into the cool, shadowy interior of the church.

He felt a little odd about being there. He had never been inside a popish church. And Chaplain Gleason had taken pains to warn them all against the black robes. Popishness was a sure path to hell, Chaplain Gleason said.

Leon shivered when he stepped inside the building, although it certainly wasn't cold in here, not even in contrast to the heat on the street.

He stood hesitantly near the doorway for a moment with his hat in his hands.

Whatever else this place was, it was awfully pretty. Like nothing Leon had ever seen before, really.

The outside of the old church was sun-dried mud and adobe brick. The inside, though, was decorated with carved wood panels, bright-colored paintings, and ornate if fading tapestries. Toward the front, there was even a little area set aside behind the pulpit that had silver and brass things—Leon wasn't sure what those items were but they were much too fancy to be called simply cups and plates and bowls—and a small, round, stained-glass window was set into the back wall where everyone could see it on Sunday mornings.

He let out a low breath that was near to being a whistle—a man didn't want to whistle in church, of course, even if it was in a popish church—and took a step forward.

Near the front there was a table with some candles and a wooden bowl on it. The bowl had a few coins in it. Up near the pulpit other candles were set up and burning. There was a scent in the air that Leon couldn't identify, but it smelled very nice. Perfumy, sort of.

There was a rail and low bench in front of the pulpit, and several women with shawls pulled over their heads were kneeling on the near side of the rail. Leon didn't know what they were doing there. There wasn't any black robe there to talk to them or anything. The women had their heads down and seemed to be muttering to themselves, and one of them was doing something with her hands, although from where he was Leon couldn't see what she was holding and manipulating so busily.

Another woman came inside and put her shawl over her head, then carried one of the candles up to the rack where the other candles were burning. She kind of curtsied and bobbed and did that funny thing with her hands like Leon had seen popists do before, then lighted her candle from one of the others and put it in the rack before she went to the rail, knelt there, and went through some rigmarole that Leon couldn't understand.

He took a step backward. Chaplain Gleason was right about just about everything. He must be right about these folks too.

"Yes, my son?"

The voice came from practically beside Leon's left ear, and the unexpected closeness of it very nearly sent him jumping straight out of his skin.

There was a black robe standing right there beside him.

Leon swallowed and groped for something to say.

The preacher smiled at him.

Chaplain Gleason had had nothing good to say about these folks, but this particular one didn't look fat or greedy. This one was tall and thin and very old. He was nearly bald, and his robe—it was really gray, not black at all—was threadbare and plain. He had a cross hung on a thong around his neck, but the cross looked like it was made out of pewter or tin instead of gold like Leon would have expected.

Leon wasn't sure if he should smile back at the black robe or run like hell.

Before Leon knew what was happening the black robe had taken Leon's hand in both his own and was grasping it warmly, still smiling at him. Leon glanced down. The black robe's skin was a pale, slightly dusky tan, not at all like Leon's darkly rich hue. The contrast seemed extreme. But the man's touch was warm and friendly.

"You must be Leon Brown," the preacher said. "We have been hoping you would come worship with us, Mr. Brown."

Mister. Leon blinked. That was just about the first time anyone had ever called him mister. Unless he wanted to count Lawyer Farr's letters, and he did not. He had been called a great many other things before, but rarely that. Mr. Ramsey the other day. Now this black robe. It was enough to make a man feel good, almost.

"I, uh . . . ."

The black robe smiled. "I am Father Felipe." The smile got wider. "Welcome, Mr. Brown."

"Father, you said?"

"You are not Catholic, Mr. Brown?"

Leon shook his head. He was still nervous in this place.

"No matter. You are welcome to worship with us. And perhaps you and I could talk sometime. About Jesus and Mary and the miracles."

Leon's nervousness increased. This black robe—Father Felipe as he called himself—certainly seemed nice enough. But Chaplain Gleason said they were all like that. What they really wanted was to get their popish hooks into Christians.

Leon wanted to pull away and leave, but Father Felipe was still holding on to his hand. And Leon had come here for a purpose, dammit.

"I was . . . I was looking for a preacher," he blurted. "For a wedding."

"The marriage ceremony is one of the great joys of the priesthood," Father Felipe said. "The joining of two people in God's love and the baptizing of their children are among the more pleasurable duties we are called upon to perform."

"Yes . . . well—"

"The lady you wish to marry. Is she here in Kazumal?" Father Felipe certainly gave every impression that the question was a sincere one, even though the whole community had to know that there was no Negro woman in town.

"She, uh, she'll be joining me, uh, later."

Father Felipe smiled and nodded. "I would be happy to perform the ceremony for you when that time comes, Mr. Brown." He was still hanging on to Leon's hand. The palm of that hand had begun to sweat.

"I . . . think I'd better be going now," Leon said uncertainly.

"Of course." Father Felipe let go of the hand and stepped closer to drape an arm over Leon's shoulders. Not very many men were tall enough to do that comfortably. And no white man had ever tried to do it before now. Father Felipe seemed quite comfortable, actually.

"If you wish, Mr. Brown, attend Mass with us. You are most welcome." He laughed. "I grant you might not understand much of our service, not being Catholic. Mass is conducted in Latin and Spanish, you see, but I would be glad to explain it to you. And God listens no matter what tongue we speak to Him in. Come. Please. Any morning at six and on Sundays also at eight and ten."

"Yeah, well. I don't know—"

"Think about it. There is no need to decide now. You are welcome anytime."

"Yeah, well, uh, thanks." Leon was twisting the brim of his hat in both hands.

"Anytime," Father Felipe assured him. He walked with Leon to the front doors and outside into the glare of the afternoon sun beside him where anyone in Kazumal might have seen the old priest with the tall black outsider.

Leon put on his hat and nodded, not sure what he ought to do now. Chaplain Gleason had said something about black robes wanting people to kiss their feet, but Leon certainly wasn't going to do that.

He settled for a handshake and another nod and hoofed it down the street in a hurry, not really sure if he should feel good about this encounter or worried by it.

At least, though, he had a preacher—priest, that is—

lined up for when Anne May got here. That was something.

He glanced toward the sinking sun and thought about the heat on the walk back home. It would already be too late to get any work done by the time he got there, and it would be more comfortable if he waited for sundown before he started the eleven-mile hike.

He decided to go along with Father Felipe's crowd and have a bit of a siesta before he headed for home.

7

Leon woke up chilled and groggy. It was amazing how cold drying sweat could feel now that the sun was gone, and his head was aching. He wasn't accustomed to naps and did not think he liked the idea now that he had tried it once.

He sat up and rubbed his face. What he needed was a drink to cut the sour taste in his throat and a wash to clear his head.

He was still in the Mexican end of town. For some reason—because of the black robe, he realized when he thought about it—he felt more comfortable here than in the white section. He had found a place behind an abandoned jacal to lie down in earlier. If he remembered correctly, there was a water trough not too far away.

He found it and drank deeply, then splashed the refreshing water over his face and neck until some of the grogginess went away and he began to feel almost human again.

It was completely dark now. He had slept longer than he intended.

Some Mexican children were playing in the street not far away. They ignored him, not at all intimidated or afraid because of his presence. Leon liked that. He stood for a few minutes watching them play. Someday, he thought, he would be able to listen to his own children shout and run at their play. It was something he looked forward to.

Now that he was awake and moving about he was not cold any longer, but he was hungry. And he hadn't yet bought the supplies he had intended to get while he was here.

He walked back through the ramshackle area that divided the two distinct neighborhoods of Kazumal, and discovered that he had slept too long. All the stores on the main street of town were closed except for the two saloons. There was nowhere he could buy something to eat, dammit, and he didn't like the thought of having to make the long walk home on an empty stomach.

Anyone else could go into one of the saloons and make a meal from the free-lunch counters. Leon knew better than to start that kind of trouble. He might be able to buy a beer out the back door of such a place, but he wouldn't be welcome inside with the white customers. And even though he might be able to buy a beer, he didn't want one. It was a taste he'd never acquired. Even during the years he spent in the army he never drank. He had always been too intent on saving his money for the future, for this future, to want to spend it on drinking with the other men of the outfit. That had made him something of a loner, but he didn't regret it. The others who left the Tenth went back to working for fifty cents a day when they were lucky enough to find work. Leon was a landowner now. A rancher. No, he had no regrets.

He did, though, have a gnawing hunger in his belly.

If he couldn't buy anything to eat in this end of town, he might still be able to find something in Father Felipe's end. He turned back that way.

Several places still showed lights and activity in the Mexican end of town, but if any of them was a store or a café, Leon could not be sure of it. None of them had signs outside telling strangers what to expect.

He chose the nearest of the lot and looked in from the doorway.

The place was a cantina, but even though it was in the Mexican end of town, it was not patronized only by Mexicans. Half a dozen white men, including the two he had seen earlier at the livery, were drinking and laughing at the bar. There were Mexicans at the bar too, and no one seemed to mind the mixture here.

Over in a corner there was a pair of fancy women, Mexican women wearing short skirts and bright rouge on their cheeks. Even while Leon watched, two of the white men swaggered over to the whores, flipped them a dollar each, and took them outside by a back door.

Leon didn't like it, but he couldn't help feel a stir of desire at the thought of the whores. It had been a very long time since he had been with a woman. Too long. Anne May was still far away.

He forced back the impulse. He had come here for food, not sex. And the last thing he needed now was that kind of trouble. A black man who so much as looked at a woman who "belonged" to the whites was practically asking for a lynching.

He backed away from the door and went on in search of a place where he might be able to buy some groceries or even a real, cooked meal.

Leon felt good. His own cooking skills were rudimentary at best. And that was putting it the most charitable way possible. For the most part he would have gotten flavor just as good if he threw out his dinner and ate the ashes from the stove when he cooked for himself.

Now, though, he felt replete, his stomach warmed from the inside out by the spicy meal he had eaten. And he hadn't even had to eat it in an alley or sitting on the ground somewhere. He had gone right inside and sat at a table, and they served him without a qualm. That was almost as nice as the meal had been.

The only part of the meal he hadn't wolfed down with genuine pleasure was the beans. He swore he would never eat beans again if he did not have to, and tonight he hadn't had to. There had been more than enough of everything else to enjoy.

He belched happily and walked up the dark street. Going home was not going to be such a . . .

A low, anguished whimper came out of an alley he was passing.

Leon stopped.

The whimper was repeated. Softer this time. Almost a

moan. It sounded like a puppy. Perhaps a puppy that had been hurt.

Leon was a sucker for puppies. For very nearly any animal, for that matter. Being around horses was one of the reasons he had enjoyed the cavalry so much.

It occurred to him that a puppy here in town would likely belong to someone. But surely no one could object if the pup was hurt and abandoned and he took it in.

He went to the alley and felt his way slowly into the intense darkness, not wanting to step on the pup if he was close. The alley was at the side of the cantina he had looked into earlier, but there were no side windows on the adobe building to let light into the narrow confinement of the passage. The frame building on the other side was dark and silent.

The whimper sounded again from a few yards away, and Leon bent low, snapping his fingers in the darkness and whispering, "Here, fella. Here. I won't hurt you. Here, fella."

He heard it again, and a slight stir of movement. It was very close now. Right . . .

His hand found the source of the sound. And recoiled.

It wasn't a pup he had touched, but a human.

His fingers came away damp and sticky.

The warmth of the meal dissipated, and Leon felt a stone-hard coldness in his belly.

Common sense told him he should get the hell out of there. Right now. If the injured man was dying . . . If anyone came along and found a black man bending over him . . .

The person whimpered again, the small sound of it driving deep into Leon's chest.

Maybe the person wasn't dying, after all. Or would die if he was left here but could be saved if somebody did something to help now.

Dammit, anyway.

Leon knelt in the dirt of the alley beside the injured person. "It's going to be all right," he whispered, not at all certain that he wasn't lying about that.

8

What Leon needed here was a light. He had tended enough wounded troopers to know that you could make things worse by moving injured persons before you knew what was wrong them them. So what he needed was a light, even if that did mean the risk of calling attention to himself in the alley.

He snapped his fingers. He had no lamp in his pockets, but he had matches and he knew where to find a candle.

"Be right back," he whispered.

He backed out of the alley and ran the block to Father Felipe's church, darted inside to grab one of the candles from a table near the entrance, and ran back out into the night again, ignoring a questioning yelp of surprise from someone inside the sanctuary.

He ran hard back to the alley and stopped there to snap a match aflame and light the candle before he returned to the dark form huddled on the ground.

When he got a look at the person in the light of the church candle, he very nearly lost his nerve and ran again.

It was a woman lying there on the ground.

A fan of long, dark hair spread over the dirt beneath her head was the only giveaway that this was a woman. Her face was so badly battered that Leon wouldn't have been able to tell otherwise. Her clothing was a tangle of shapeless rags, although closer inspection showed that the lower mass of rags was a heavy skirt.

Her lips were split and an ugly bruise covered most of the left side of her face. Her left eye was swollen closed. One large, intensely black disk stared dully up at him from the slit that should have been her right eye. Her mouth and nose were bleeding profusely, but those wounds were superficial.

What concerned Leon was that she was huddled into a tight ball, her knees drawn toward her chest, and she had both arms wrapped tight over her stomach. Whoever did this to her probably kicked her after she was knocked down. She might very well be bleeding inside her belly. If that was so, there was nothing Leon or anyone else could do for her.

He set the candle on a discarded crate and knelt at her side.

He removed the bright-yellow bandanna from his hip pocket and very gently wiped her face with it, removing some of the blood. He smiled at her.

"Don't be frightened. I won't hurt you." He smiled again. "I'm not doing a very good job of this. Wait a minute. Be right back."

He went out into the street and drenched the bandanna in a nearby water trough, then hurried back to the woman.

"Does that feel better?" he asked as he bathed her face with the wet cloth. "You look better, that's for sure."

She didn't. Once the blood was removed, he could see the extent of her injuries. He suspected that she hadn't been pretty to begin with, and now she looked terrible. He doubted that her nose would ever be quite the same again, and there would probably be scarring on the left side of her face. There was a deep gash over her cheek-bone where the flesh had split almost to the bone from a blow, and that one was certain to leave an unpleasant scar.

She was dark-complexioned for a Mexican. It was difficult to tell what her features had been like before this happened to her, but her bone structure was heavy and her brows thick.

"Are you hurting here? Can you speak English?" He tried to pull her hands away from her stomach, but she resisted him. He didn't force it, instead bathing her face again and giving her time to relax the protective position if she could.

Leon heard the approach of hesitant footsteps, and he went cold. If someone thought . . .

"Can you speak?"

The woman blinked but didn't answer.

"Mr. Brown."

Father Felipe was at the mouth of the alley. Leon felt a rush of relief. Surely the priest would understand.

Father Felipe hurried to join him, kneeling beside the woman.

"I didn't . . . I found her like this, Father. I swear I did."

"It is all right, my son. Help me. We will take her to the church."

"I don't think we should move her, Father. See the way she's holding herself? She could be hurt inside."

Father Felipe nodded. "As you think best, Mr. Brown."

"Father, I don't know what to think." He settled for wiping the woman's face again with the now-drying, blood-encrusted bandanna.

The woman's battered lips moved. It was painful just to watch as the torn flesh was manipulated. The slight movements of her whispered speech caused fresh blood to flow. Leon wiped it away as gently as he could.

The words, whatever they were, were in Spanish.

Father Felipe smiled and ran his hand lightly across her forehead. "She says she does not need the last rites, thank God," he said.

"Is that good?"

"That is very good. She hurts, but she says she felt nothing tear. She will live."

"Good."

"Give me . . . little time . . . I be fine now," the woman whispered.

Leon doubted that, but he admired her attitude about it. He went back out to the water trough, washed the blood out of his bandanna, and brought it back to bathe her face again.

"That feels good," she said, then added something else in Spanish.

Father Felipe smiled but didn't translate for Leon's benefit.

"We will give her a little time," he said, "then if you would help me move her . . . ?"

"Sure, Father."

The woman closed her eyes, and her breathing deepened. Leon didn't think she was quite asleep, but she was close to it, mustering her strength in rest. He thought it was a good sign that her legs relaxed and her arms drew slightly away from the tight hold she had been maintaining across her stomach.

Father Felipe motioned for Leon to back away and let her rest. The priest sat on an upturned beer cask and patted another one next to him where Leon could sit. "We will give her a little time."

Leon nodded. "Shouldn't we, uh, call the town marshal or something?"

Father Felipe looked sad. "No, Mr. Brown. Not for this one, I fear."

Leon raised an eyebrow.

"Surely you must know what it is to be an outcast, Mr. Brown?" the priest suggested.

Leon looked at the woman who was lying on the ground nearby, and Father Felipe nodded.

"Her name is Manuela, Mr. Brown. She is half of our people but half Apache too. A daughter of rape, you see. It was only by a miracle that her mother escaped the raiders alive. She returned to us with child, and Manuela was born. I think sometimes it would have been a mercy if the child had not survived. But it is not my place to question God's wisdom about this, Mr. Brown.

"Manuela has no name but one. She has no people. Her mother died when Manuela was still a child." He sighed. "We are a poor people, Mr. Brown. We were even poorer then, before so many of the Anglos came. Manuela survived as best she could. She is a *puta*. A woman of bad repute. You understand what I mean, Mr. Brown?"

"Sure, but—"

"Manuela is not pretty, Mr. Brown. The less-decent

Anglos of Kazumal use her. The ones who delight in another's pain, Mr. Brown. That is probably what happened to her tonight.'' The old priest shook his head. ''A *puta* here, Mr. Brown, earns half a dollar for her services.''

Leon was surprised that a priest would know about such things, but he didn't interrupt.

''A very pretty *puta,* very young, she can earn as much as a dollar. Manuela is paid twenty-five cents. Sometimes less. The men who summon her think this is funny. It is another form of cruelty. Manuela does what they require. It is what she must do to survive. And my own people''— he shrugged—''I do what I can, but they look down on her because of her Indio blood. They fear the Apache who have killed so many for so long, and because they fear the Apache, they sometimes vent their fears on this woman who will never know who her father was.''

''Well, Father, that isn't her fault.''

''Of course it is not, but fear often overcomes reason, Mr. Brown. Surely you have seen this when you walk among the Anglos.''

''Fear, Father? I've never done anything to—''

''That does not matter, Mr. Brown. Fear is beyond reason. It is not hate you see in those faces but fear. Just as Manuela sees it among the people here. We fear what we do not know. We fear what is different.'' He smiled. ''Do not reject what I am telling you, Mr. Brown, until you have thought about it.''

''Maybe I'll do that. Just maybe I will.''

The woman's one good eye opened, and she said something in Spanish.

''Will you help me with her, Mr. Brown?''

''Of course.''

Between them the old priest and the black man lifted Manuela and carried her down the street to the church. They took her through the sanctuary to a small room in back where a robe much fancier than Father Felipe's everyday gray one was hanging on a peg. That and a crucifix on the wall were the only decorations. A bench was the only furniture. They placed her on the bench, and

Father Felipe wadded the ornate robe to serve as a pillow for the injured woman.

"I will take care of her now, my son."

"Is there anything I can do?"

"Nothing, Mr. Brown. I will do what I can." He shrugged as if to add that it would be little under the circumstances.

Leon stood over the woman for a moment, looking down at her. Her one good eye stared back up at him, bright and birdlike now. She didn't try to speak.

Leon sighed. This Manuela, it seemed, had drawn an even shittier deal than he had. At least he wasn't letting people abuse him for a living.

On an impulse Leon reached into his pocket. He pulled out a silver dollar, leaned down, and pressed it into her palm.

"I hope . . . I hope you get to feeling better, ma'am."

He turned and hurried out of the church and into the night. It was going to be very late before he got home.

9

Leon was footsore and discouraged. He had discovered a small group of his cattle finally. But it had taken three days of walking over the dry, sprawling land that was supposed to become his empire, and now that he had found them, there was nothing he could do with them.

Fourteen head of cattle—eight cows with three half-grown calves, two small calves, and one aging steer—were holed up in the dense undergrowth of the coulee some fourteen or fifteen miles south of the house. Leon wasn't sure that the land was his own. In fact, he doubted that it was. Still, the maps Farr sent him through the mail showed that there was only unclaimed land to the south of his, so that probably made no difference.

The problem was that a lone man afoot can't do anything with loose cattle except find them. He certainly can't capture or herd them by himself without a horse.

The frustrations of his situation seemed even more difficult to bear now that he had actually found some of the cattle he bought with the ranch.

He sat wearily on a crumbling rock atop a small hillock and took a sip of tepid water from the bottle he had taken to carrying with him on his searches. Water was scarce in this country, and he had discovered already that it was uncomfortable at best to wander far without taking the water bottle with him.

He held the water in his mouth for a moment to savor the feel of it on his tongue and throat, then allowed the life-giving fluid to trickle very slowly down.

"That's better," he said to the solitary cloud that floated far overhead in the bright Arizona sky.

The cattle with the bold 3H brand on their hips were lying in the scant shade of the brush, rechewing whatever it was they had found to eat in the sparse growth of this country. Leon wished he could say the same about himself. Shade alone would be welcome. He tugged the brim of his hat lower to block the sun.

Off in the distance he could see dust rising. Something was moving out there three, four miles away.

Apaches? It was not impossible. The San Carlos Agency reservation was well to the north, but that meant nothing. The bronchos could be anywhere from Mexico to Utah and from west Texas all the way across nearly to California. The unrepentant wild bands still went where they pleased and raided wherever they went.

Leon stayed where he was. Even a broncho Apache wouldn't be looking for one man on foot in this country. He'd be safe enough as long as he stayed immobile. It's movement that draws the eye, not color or shape.

The dust rise came closer. Leon could make out horses moving at a trot. The animals were riderless, and unless there were horsemen riding back in the dust where he couldn't yet see them, the herd was undriven.

They came within a mile. He was sure now that they were running loose. There was certainly nothing strange about that. This was, after all, open range. Anyone was free to graze stock on unclaimed land.

As the herd came even closer, though, he could see too that this bunch was unkempt. Their tails streamed long and untrimmed behind them as they moved. No cowman Leon knew of and certainly no cavalry trooper ever let a horse's tail grow so lengthy and tangled.

The herd—there were thirty-five or forty horses in the bunch—reached the coulee where Leon's few cattle were resting. They dropped down into it, sliding down the bank one by one and raising up still more dust.

The manes of the horses were every bit as tangled and burr-choked as their tails.

Excitement began to fill Leon's chest, and he had to hold it back with effort or he might have jumped to his feet before the last mare in line dropped out of sight beneath the near bank of the coulee.

These were wild horses. Mustangs, they called them over in Texas when the Tenth was working out of Fort Davis. Unbranded, unclaimed, free running bronco horses that were every bit as wild as the broncho Apaches.

A grin began to spread across Leon's dark, sweat-streaked face.

Mustangs belonged to any man who could capture and brand them.

He shifted his seat on the rock and began a slow, patient vigil. The solution to Leon's transportation problems might just be in sight.

10

Leon was feeling good. Awfully good. It had taken him days of hiking and nights of spying, but he was finally beginning to learn and anticipate the habits of the mustang herd.

There were actually thirty-seven head in the bunch.

And there were only two places where the herd could water.

One of these was a rock *tinaja* catch pond hidden against the side of a dry, barren hill where no one would possibly think to find water. If the mustangs hadn't led him there, Leon would've never found it on his own.

The other was a pond and thin trickle of stream that flowed only a few yards before it disappeared into the sand again in the bottom of the coulee where he had first found his cattle. That water would be the reason the cattle had rested there too, he realized now.

Leon had learned early on that too much time and effort were wasted if he tried to sleep at home each night and walk out again each morning in time to look for the mustangs. The coulee was at the north end of their territory. The southern extent of the land they used was more than thirty miles from the house, and he wanted no part of having to walk that twice a day. Instead, he carried food with him and a blanket and depended on the pond in the coulee for his water. The nights were chill and fireless, but he didn't mind that. He had slept under much worse conditions when the Tenth was on campaign, particularly during the awful winter patrols.

He spent four days doing nothing but observing the

wild, roaming horses, becoming acquainted with their habits and patterns.

He spent two more days in hard labor at the *tinaja*. It was grueling work, but he enjoyed doing it. It was work he was doing for himself and for Anne May and not just to meet some officer's whim.

He worked practically from dawn to dark, finding, lifting, and carrying stones and setting them into a dry wall that he slowly erected around the pool of water.

What he had to do was reduce the water sources for the horse herd to one. He had to force them to water from now on only in the steep-sided coulee.

By the morning of the third day he had the *tinaja* walled off so that only birds or very small animals could get to it.

The mustangs were aware of him by now, of course. Leon had been sleeping near the *tinaja* nightly ever since he began this phase of his plan, and the horses shied from his presence. They still ranged close to the *tinaja* once each day, shortly after dawn, but they no longer tried to approach it. They stayed a good half-mile out, whinnying and complaining but not coming closer to the water where the man worked.

Leon looked at them and grinned.

"You're gonna be mine," he told them happily.

Once the *tinaja* was safely walled away from the mustangs, Leon moved his camp north.

This time he didn't dare sleep close to the pond and stream. He couldn't risk driving the mustangs completely out of the country in search of new water sources. He set up camp several miles away from the coulee pond and spent two days observing the newly enforced changes in the habits of the horse herd.

Since they could no longer depend on the *tinaja* for water, they came now twice daily to the coulee to drink. Once in the evening just at dusk. Again in the morning after a night of grazing. During the day they continued their wandering, swinging south from the coulee on long sweeps that covered twenty miles or more in a wide circle before returning to the pond.

Leon smiled. He was patient. He knew now how to handle it.

He woke with the dawn, walked to the top of a small promontory, and sat down to wait.

In the distance he could see the scruffy, scarred old mare who led the herd reach the wall of the coulee and pause there for a moment before dropping down the path out of sight. The others followed her without hesitation.

That was one thing that had surprised Leon, even after all the years he spent living and working with the Tenth's horses. He really expected that the stallion of the bunch would be their leader.

The male was a stock black with a splash of white on his underbelly. The stud showed the scars of innumerable battles in the past, and he had driven all the other males except a few very young colts out of his band. Most of the herd consisted of mares and fillies.

Yet it was the ancient, ugly brown mare that was the day-to-day leader of the herd.

Leon waited patiently for the bunch to drink their fill from the pond. After forty-five minutes or so, they filed back out of the coulee, scrambling for the top of the wall on the path they always used and drifting toward the southwest at a slow trot, the brown mare again in the lead.

Leon stayed where he was until the mustangs were out of sight and he could barely see the dust of their passage.

Then with a grunt of anticipation he stood, his knee joints popping, and started down toward the coulee.

11

He spent an entire day resting when the last of the "easy" part was done.

Everything was ready at the coulee. He had built another wall below the pond and the last, faint dampness where the short stream sank into the sand. The dry stone wall extended from one steep coulee bank to the other, effectively blocking any exit from the wash in that direction.

Above the pond, between it and the place where the horses twice daily used the path they had eroded in the natural wall of the coulee, he had positioned stout cedar posts and laced them with brush torn from the upper end of the coulee—the cattle had not liked having their resting place disturbed—until only a gap of eight or ten feet remained open through which the mustangs could pass to reach the pond.

Leon had cut the stoutest poles he could find and placed them beside this "gate."

Once he had the mustangs inside his trap around their water source, he only needed to pull the hidden poles across the gap, and the horses would be his.

He was hoping the mustangs would go into the trap on their own. He frankly doubted they would. At Fort Stockton once he had listened while an old horse hunter—a white man who had not deigned to acknowledge that a raggedy-ass, buffalo soldier private was listening in but who nevertheless spoke a little louder so even the eavesdropper could admire the man's many feats—was bragging about his prowess.

So Leon thought he knew what would have to be done.

He hoped he was wrong. He hoped the herd would walk inside and conveniently trap themselves.

He didn't trust himself to wake in time to get into position, so he stayed up through the night and a few hours before dawn crept down into the coulee and hid himself in the brush he had piled as camouflage against the fence.

He wished he had thought to bring a blanket with him. It was chilly and he was shivering, but it was too late now to go back to camp.

He lay where he was, ears tuned to the faintest sound.

The sun came up and gradually began to warm the bottom of the coulee. This was the only really comfortable time of day, the short period between the cold of the night and the furnace heat of the daylight. Leon stretched and stopped his shivering.

He smiled when he felt faint vibrations in the earth. A moment later he heard the approach of hoofbeats.

They were coming.

A dozen feet over his head he could hear the mustangs cross the sandy flat to the edge of the coulee.

They stopped, damn them.

He heard a whuff of air as one of them snorted.

It would be that damned old brown mare. She sensed something, damn her, or smelled something.

Another horse fluttered its nostrils and whinnied.

Hell, but he wished he could see what was going on up there.

There was an abrupt squeal and a crash of hard hooves against the earth as two of the mustangs argued about something. Then another squeal and the herd broke into a pounding run toward the south.

The damn brown was not letting them come to the water.

Leon groaned and stood, brushing the sand off himself.

He knew where they would be going now. They would be trying the *tinaja* again. He could cut straight across and catch them there.

Not too fast, though. He didn't want to get ahead of them. He had to come in behind them. He had to push them into their own natural pattern in the circle of their normal route. He had to get behind them, let them know he was following, and force them to move away from him now.

Walking them down, that old man had called it.

Leon shuddered just from thinking about it. He had hoped to avoid this, but now he had to do it.

If he gave the herd time to think—if horses thought— if he gave them time to react to anything but the instinct of flight, they would very likely drift away to another range and look for other water.

From now until either the horses dropped or he did, he was going to have to be behind them, alarming them, keeping them moving and reacting in fear of man. He had to keep them circling back to this one pond, running always in front of him, until they had to either come to water inside the trap or die.

And if for even a few hours Leon lay down to sleep or stopped his slow, dogged foot pursuit of the horse band, they would have time to recover from their instinctive flight and leave this country.

"Damn you, anyhow," he said aloud as he climbed the bank to the sandy flat and got ready to walk south toward the *tinaja* so many miles away.

Leon staggered, righted himself, and licked his lips with a tongue that was nearly as dry as his lips were.

Yesterday he had tripped and fallen on the damned water bottle. Now he could only reach water himself when the herd's swing brought him close to the pond or to the *tinaja*.

The horses were in worse shape. They could only reach water at the pond, but even on this third day of the pursuit the stinking bitch of a brown mare wouldn't let them down into the damned coulee.

The old mare was a fighter. He could get close enough to them now to see that. She stood at the top of the path into the coulee and fought off any horse that wanted to give up and go to water, man or no man.

"Old bitch," Leon mumbled aloud. He hoped the

stinking brown died of thirst. Then maybe he could catch the rest of them.

But he didn't hope that either, damn her. A horse with that much heart would be something to have if she could ever be tamed.

"Old bitch," he said again.

He was wearing them down, though.

That first day they boogered and ran whenever he came in sight, no matter how far away he was. They outran him easily and could stop whenever they wished to graze and take some small amount of moisture from their browse.

But that had been at first.

Always Leon was trudging slowly behind them. Never running. Just walking. He wished now he had been in the damned infantry and was used to this shit. Or at least had boots intended for walking. Except the damned infantry wore shoes. Leon was proud of his boots. He was . . .

He shook his head. His thoughts were wandering again. He'd caught himself doing that several times today, and it scared him. He had to keep his senses, dammit, or the mustangs would get away.

They were ahead of him right now. Not more than a hundred yards in front and staring nervously back toward this human thing that kept after them every day and all through each night.

They no longer ran in front of him. They hadn't the strength for that. Now the herd was only capable of walking barely faster than he was.

"Damn you," he shouted at them.

The stallion squealed and pawed futilely at the earth, but it didn't charge him. The brown mare was the leader, but the stud horse was the defender of the band.

Leon picked up a rock and flung it at the horse. The stone fell far short, of course, but the stallion shied and stumbled into an agonized trot.

"Don't you dumb bastards know to quit?" Leon shouted after them. And stumbled on behind them.

They were only a few miles from the coulee again.

Each circle carried them a dozen miles. That was an improvement, though. When they began, each circle was twice that long.

Now the bastards were coming more and more often within scent of the pond and the trap that waited for them there.

"Dumb bastards," Leon complained.

He passed the carcass of a foal that had gone down yesterday. The filly was not more than four, five months old and had not been strong enough to keep up with the herd. Something, birds or rodents or coyotes, had been at the body since Leon passed it on the last circle, and it was beginning to bloat and stink.

Up ahead he could see another of the younger horses, a colt that he particularly liked, stagger and drop to its knees. It fought its way back onto its legs and walked on, trailing the rest of the herd and closer to Leon now than to its dam.

Within a mile Leon caught up to the colt and passed it. The yearling's eyes were dull and its coat grimed with caked sweat and dust.

Leon walked on behind the rest of the herd, and the colt struggled to follow.

"Damn you," Leon shouted.

Behind him the colt continued trying to follow its herd even though the man walked between it and them.

Leon's knees buckled. He sat down hard in the sand. He wanted to cry.

The old bitch of a mare was going down the path.

She led the way and the others followed. Many of them fell, too weak to negotiate the path that was so familiar to them. They weaved and wobbled as they regained their feet and passed through the gate to reach the pond.

Leon followed them down. He was only a few feet behind them now. They no longer cared. At this point he barely cared himself.

He went to the gate and it took all the strength he had left to pick up a pole and slide it into place.

Then he had to take the pole down again so the yearling that had been behind him could get in to the life-giving relief of the water it had been so long denied.

The colt fell at the foot of the path and tried to find its legs again.

Leon walked back and helped the near-dead yearling up. He pushed it toward the gate. The young horse was too far gone to object to the handling.

He shoved it inside and fell to his knees, as close to being dead as the damned horses were.

Sobbing but dry-eyed—he was too parched to spare the moisture tears would take, he was sure—he began pulling the poles across the gap in the fence.

The mustangs were his, damn them.

Including the stubborn, stupid old bitch of a brown mare.

God, but he hated that horse. God, but he hoped he could break her.

A man could learn to love a horse with that much heart.

Leon collapsed in the shade of the coulee wall. He was asleep almost before he felt the sand.

12

Leon couldn't help feeling a bit of pride as he rode into
Jud Ramsey's yard. He was astride the brown mare. The
old bitch had been hard to gentle, but the work had been
worthwhile. Even cleaned up and the burrs trimmed out
of her hair, she was an ugly thing. But she had sense and
bottom and a gait that was easy on the tailbone. Which
was a good thing, since all he had for a saddle was a
piece of castoff blanket tied around her middle. Breaking
her without a saddle had been a chore, and Leon was
hoping he wouldn't have to do the same with all the rest
of the horses he had captured.

"Mr. Brown." Ramsey came out of his house, larger
and much nicer than the old Harrold place.

"Mr. Ramsey." Leon touched the brim of his hat but
remained on the mare.

"Get down, please. Coffee?"

Leon was overwhelmed by the offer. It was a simple-
enough thing, probably, but it was a white man who extended the invitation. From the way Ramsey was acting,
motioning him toward the door of his home, the man was
even expecting Leon to go inside the house.

Leon slid off the mare's back and tied her to a post set
in front of Ramsey's porch. "That's kind of you, Mr.
Ramsey."

"*De nada.*" Ramsey held the door open, and Leon
went in. "You've been away. I, uh, stopped by your
place a couple times these past few weeks. Couldn't seem
to find you home."

Leon took his hat off and wiped his feet on a rag rug
in front of the door. He felt a trifle uncomfortable here.

But there was no hint in Ramsey's tone of voice that the man might be baiting him. Setting him up for a cruel joke. Ramsey seemed entirely sincere.

"I've been down south," Leon said. "On the public land."

"Mmm." Ramsey motioned Leon to a seat at his table, poured two cups of steaming coffee, and sat across the table from Leon. The aroma of the coffee, the first Leon had had since he mustered out at Larned, was heady. The taste of it was even better.

"The reason I stopped by," Ramsey was saying, "was that I was remiss the last time I saw you. I should have offered you the loan of a horse. Heard in town afterward that that idiot Brenmere wouldn't sell you one."

Leon smiled grimly over the rim of his cup. "Oh, he would've sold one."

"Yes. So I heard. Heard the price he wanted too. I should've loaned you one, but I didn't think. I see you found one, though."

Leon grinned and told Ramsey where he had gotten his mare.

"Good Lord. You're serious? Excuse me. Of course you are. And you walked them down? Incredible." He shook his head. "I've heard of it before, that. But I never heard of fewer than four people managing it. Frankly, Mr. Brown, I'd always thought the stories apocryphal. That is—"

"I know what it means, Mr. Ramsey."

"Yes, uh, sorry." Ramsey smiled. "Forgive me, Mr. Brown, but I'm not entirely comfortable this evening."

"I could leave if—"

"No," Ramsey said quickly. "It isn't you, Mr. Brown. The problem is mine. What the neighbors would think and all that." He smiled again, then laughed aloud. "Now that I think about it, Mr. Brown, you are the neighbor, aren't you?"

Leon chuckled. He took another swallow of coffee. It was stale and acid and utterly delicious after being so long without it.

"Since you don't need the use of a horse, Mr. Brown, what can I do to be neighborly?"

"I didn't come asking for handouts, Mr. Ramsey. But there is something . . ."

"If I can help, I will." Ramsey got up and refilled both cups.

"I need to buy some rope, Mr. Ramsey. And an old saddle if you have one to spare. I've been making do, of course. And I could go into town and see what I can find there. But I happened to think . . . I mean, if there is any work you need done, anything at all, I'd be glad to trade sweat for any equipment you no longer need."

Ramsey pulled at his chin, and for a moment Leon thought he was looking for a way to refuse the request. Then he realized that Ramsey must have been thinking of offering the needed items as a loan but rejected that idea out of consideration for Leon's pride. "I could use your help driving some beefs of mine to Douglas, Mr. Brown. Would you consider that a fair exchange?"

"More than fair, Mr. Ramsey."

The neighbor nodded. "Good. It's too much for one man to handle. I was afraid I might have to ask one of the Tucker boys to help me."

"Tucker?"

"You haven't met them yet? You will. They have holdings just west of yours. They . . . Well, never mind. I shouldn't prejudge them. That wouldn't be fair at all."

"No, I'm sure it wouldn't." Ramsey had made his point rather well, Leon thought, for a man who was careful to say nothing bad about a neighbor. "They have sons, you say?"

"That's right. Five boys and two girls and some assorted uncles and cousins on the place now and then. Large family. Been here a long time by whi . . . , uh, Anglo standards."

Leon smiled. "It's okay to say it, Mr. Ramsey. I know what white men are."

"Yes. I suppose you do." Ramsey's smile was a little nervous again.

"Comes to that, Mr. Ramsey, it's all right for you to

say that I'm colored or black. That's plain fact. I don't find it offensive. Or shameful, for that matter.''

Ramsey smiled again, the expression easier this time. ''Thank you, Mr. Brown.''

''If it helps any, Mr. Ramsey, I'm kinda new at this too. And a little uncomfortable.'' Leon drained his cup and stood to carry it to the dry sink. ''Thank you for the coffee, Mr. Ramsey. And for everything else.''

''*De nada,*'' Ramsey said again. He stood. ''Why don't we go out to the barn and see what you need from that mess I keep out there.''

13

The work of breaking the horses went much more quickly after Leon had a saddle, ropes, and hackamore to work with. The make-do equipment had made the job of taming the mare much harder than it should have been.

As soon as the herd was gentled enough, Leon and the brown mare drove them back to the 3H to the corrals he had rebuilt. The old stallion he turned loose. The younger males he gelded and broke. The mares and fillies he gentled also. When he was done, he had twenty-three fairly decent mares including the excellent brown and eleven geldings. He had kept one three-year-old stallion whole in the hope of increasing his horse herd. Horses were not the reason he had come here, but there might be a market for them.

Once he was satisfied that the now-gentled mustangs would stay close to home, he went back to Ramsey's place. He hadn't seen his neighbor in some weeks.

"You're done so soon?" Ramsey asked over coffee. "That seems awfully quick work for so many horses."

"Plenty of practice," Leon said with a smile. "The Ninth and the Tenth didn't exactly get the pick of the litter when Remount was passing out horses. I kinda had a way with the bad ones, so they had me doing a lot of it."

"I'll remember that if I need some horses broken. Pass the word around too if you like."

"I'd appreciate that, Mr. Ramsey."

"I'll do it then."

"One thing I wanted to ask, Mr. Ramsey. When you take your cows south, will you be needing a remuda?"

"Certainly."

"What I had in mind, if it wouldn't be an imposition, was that we might use my geldings for the remuda. The work would be good for them, and I could maybe sell them in Douglas once we didn't need them anymore."

"That's perfect, Mr. Brown. It would save us the trouble of having to drive loose horses home."

"That's what I was thinking."

"We'll do that. When would you like to leave, Mr. Brown?"

"Anytime you say."

"Monday next suit you?"

Leon grinned. "That will be just fine, Mr. Ramsey. If you'll let me know when Monday is supposed to be. I've kinda lost track of the days lately."

"Five days from now, Mr. Brown. That would give me time to bring in the steers I want to sell."

Leon nodded. The coffee this time was fresher than it had been on his last visit here. He was already thinking that if he got a fair price for the geldings he might buy some for himself. After all, if Ramsey came to call again, it would only be proper to be able to offer the man a cup in return for his kindness.

"I'll be here in five days then, Mr. Ramsey. Have the remuda here before first light if that suits you."

"Good enough."

Ramsey reached across the kitchen table and offered his hand on it.

This was working out, Leon thought when he rode back to his home. It would be just perfect when Anne May got here. He wondered what had happened to her letter. He would have to ride to Kazumal and check at the post office before he left for Douglas. It wouldn't do for Anne May to arrive while he was off on the drive south. He was definitely going to have to check on that before he left.

14

The drive to Douglas was a pleasure for Leon if something of a trial for him too.

Jud Ramsey's cattle were fat, stocky things, docile and slow unlike the long-legged, half-wild longhorns of Spanish breeding Leon was used to seeing, if sometimes stupid and difficult on the trail. Leon had never driven cattle before and had much to learn. At night the beefs did not have to be constantly herded—or at least so Ramsey said—and could be bedded on the bottom of a convenient swale until morning.

"They'll be all right," Ramsey said. "They've had water and their bellies are full. They aren't a flighty bunch anyway." He motioned toward the slope of a small rise overlooking the bedding ground for the cattle. "We can set up a camp over there."

Leon nodded and went to work bringing in wood for a fire. It surprised him that Ramsey pitched in and helped establish the camp for the two of them. Leon's experience with the white officers in the Tenth—there were no officers except white ones, of course—was that the men did the work while the officers watched, and as a sort of hired hand on this drive, Leon assumed he would be considered the "man" and Ramsey an officer. Apparently his neighbor didn't see it that way, though.

Ramsey cooked their dinner too—slabs of fresh beef and tallow-fried potatoes. It was the best meal Leon had had since he came to Arizona.

"Don't start killing your own beefs, Mr. Brown," Ramsey told him when he mentioned that fact. "There's plenty of game when you need meat. Deer, desert big-horns, like that."

"I thought of that, Mr. Ramsey, but I have no rifle. Just this Colt."

Ramsey grunted. "Hell, I can loan you the use of one anytime you need it. Come to think of it, I have a spare Springfield at home. You can have it. Remind me when we get back."

"I couldn't—"

"Bullshit. The rifle's public property anyhow. Belongs to you as much as it does to me. The army passed them out a couple years ago like free beer at a political debate. The idea was to arm everybody against Indian attack. What they are are some of the old .50-70 trapdoors that went obsolete when the army went over to the .45-70 cartridge."

Leon nodded. He was certainly familiar with the old model Springfields. "Thank you, Mr. Ramsey."

"De nada." Ramsey finished his meal and began scrubbing their plates.

"I can do that, Mr. Ramsey."

"Aw, I'm half done already. Why don't you take a look and see that those steers aren't making a liar of me."

Leon walked out into the evening. The cattle seemed content enough, most of them picking at the grass in the bottom where they were bedded, the rest already lying down. A coyote yapped in the distance, and somewhere closer he could hear the flutter of wings. Bats, perhaps, or an owl. Leon couldn't decide which. He cocked his head and paid attention. Bats. The sound of the flapping was harder and sharper than the soft flow of an owl's wings. He smiled and went back to the camp. Ramsey had already kicked the fire apart. The warmth of it would have been welcome through the night, but its light would have been too much of a beacon for any wandering Indians.

"Nice night," Leon observed.

"They nearly all are. Coffee? There's enough for each of us to have one last cup."

"Thanks." Leon curled his hands around the tin cup and leaned lower to take in the aroma of the beverage.

"Mind if I ask you something, Mr. Brown?"

"Of course not."

"You, uh, aren't too familiar with cattle, are you?"

Leon chuckled. "It shows that bad?"

"I didn't say that."

"But?"

Ramsey grinned. "But yes, it does."

Leon smiled back at the friendly neighbor. "I'll learn."

"True. It just seems odd that you would want to go into the cattle business."

"Been a dream of mine for a long time." Leon sipped the marvelous coffee and paused for a moment with his nose in the steam rising from its dark surface. "When I was a kid, Mr. Ramsey, I worked in the stockyards in Kansas City. I was just a kick-around pickaninny, you understand. But I'd see those cattlemen come in with their big hats and their fancy boots and all that money in their pockets, and I'd think, God, wouldn't it be fine to be able to act like that." He laughed. "Me in my bare feet, calf-deep in muck and manure, and holes in my britches, but I thought that anyway. Then I went in the army and they taught me that I could stand as tall as any man, and I got to thinking, Why not? Why couldn't I do something about it other than wish? So I saved my money, and here I am."

"So you are, Mr. Brown. No regrets?"

"Not a one." Leon tilted his head back and looked toward the stars that were bright overhead. "Not tonight."

"You never married?"

Leon grinned. "Not yet. But I'm gonna."

"You sound like you have someone in mind already."

"Oh, yes. Her name's Anne May Arbister, and we've been keeping company a long time. Whenever I could get leave to go see her. Sometimes she'd come see me wherever I was posted at the time. We've had an understanding between us for quite a while now."

"I'm happy for you, Mr. Brown." Ramsey stared off

into the night, his eyes distant and unfocused. Leon guessed that the man was thinking of his own family now dead and gone.

"You had children, you said?"

"Yes." Ramsey didn't elaborate, and Leon didn't want to press the point if Ramsey found it uncomfortable to talk about.

After a few minutes Ramsey shook himself and looked at Leon again. "You don't know all that much about cows yet, but I have no fault with you when it comes to horses. That mustang I was using this afternoon has an awfully good handle on him for such a green horse."

"Thank you, Mr. Ramsey. That's one of the things we sure wanted in a mount, in the Tenth. Can't have some crazy animal carrying you where you don't want to be when there's arrows and bullets coming out of the sky."

"You saw action, then?"

"Lord, I reckon. More than a sane man would ever want to. West Texas, New Mexico, the I.T., Kansas. I'm glad to be done with all of that now."

"I would think so." Ramsey finished his coffee, dumped the grounds, and wiped the cup out with a handful of grass. "Funny how the papers never say all that much about the colored units fighting."

Leon laughed. "We kinda noticed that ourselves. I won't say that we didn't mind, but we did get used to it."

"That time I was telling you about? Over in Texas before I moved? The newspaper in El Paso carried an item that a cavalry patrol had driven the raiders away from my place, but the story never mentioned what unit it was that saved us. In the same issue of the paper there was a story about a fight down on the border. That one was full of names and unit designations. You'd have thought the fellow writing the story was getting paid extra for every name and number he put in."

Leon laughed again. "The Twelfth that would've been?"

"Maybe. I don't remember for sure now."

"Lord, there was times we fought more with the

Twelfth than we did with the Indians. They got over that after a time, though. Turned out us darkies weren't so easy to whip as we were supposed to be.''

Ramsey chuckled. ''There are all kinds of fights, aren't there, Mr. Brown?''

''Yes, but I suppose if you can come out of each of them breathing, you're ahead of the game.''

Ramsey stood and brushed off the seat of his trousers. ''I think I'll check the horses, and then turn in. I'm getting a little long in the tooth for full days in the saddle.''

''You do that, Mr. Ramsey. I'll sit up and keep watch for a while.''

''Good night, Mr. Brown.''

Leon leaned back and sighed. It was a good night, he decided.

15

Douglas was several times the size of Kazumal and many times more prosperous. What it might have been like before the coming of the railroad Leon couldn't imagine, but now it was a bustling community of several thousand.

Shipping pens containing cattle, horses, and a sea of sheep were spread out along the rails downwind from the depot and main business district.

"This is something, isn't it?" Leon had visions of a hot, cooked meal and a chance to do some shopping if he was able to sell the geldings.

"Fine indeed," Ramsey agreed. "If you don't mind, Mr. Brown, I'll ride on ahead and see about a buyer while you stay here with the stock. The fool critters are apt to mix in with any herd they see if they aren't watched now."

"My pleasure, Mr. Ramsey."

Leon sat loose and easy on the back of a short, cat-footed roan that was nearly as nicely gaited as the old bitch mare, and waited patiently while Ramsey rode ahead, angling not for the shipping pens but for the center of town.

Leon decided it was a good thing Ramsey was in charge now. Leon would've had no idea where to look for a potential buyer. He thought perhaps he should ask Ramsey for advice about the haggling when he went to sell the horses.

Ramsey's steers seemed content enough in the glare of the sunshine. The experienced rancher had stopped them early in the morning to let the beef eat their fill before they came close to town, where practically no grass remained. Leon had observed without comment but tucked the information away against future need. That was the sort of thing that made Jud Ramsey a cowman and Leon Brown a raw recruit in this business.

It was nearly dark before Ramsey returned. His expression was grim, not at all what Leon would have expected.

"Couldn't find a buyer for the cows, Mr. Ramsey?"

"Oh, I found a buyer for them, all right. For your horses too if the price seems acceptable to you. That isn't . . . that isn't what's troubling me."

Leon raised an eyebrow.

"I went by the pens, Mr. Brown. To see where we needed to bring the stock. There are . . . I'm sorry to say this, but there are ten head of 3H beef in one of those pens."

"The 3H? But that's . . . !" Leon felt a coldness in his stomach.

The 3H was his brand.

"You must be mistaken, Mr. Ramsey."

"I am sorry, Mr. Brown. You'll want to look for yourself, of course."

Leon's first thought was to spur the roan into a run for the shipping pens. He held it back, though. Ramsey would need his help moving the steers and the geldings. They were bound for the shipping pens.

"I took the liberty of sending for the town marshal, Mr. Brown. He should join us at the pens."

Leon nodded. "If you don't mind, Mr. Ramsey . . ."

"We'll push them in quick as we can."

The two men wheeled their horses in opposite directions to pick up the herd and drive them down toward the loading pens.

16

The Douglas lawdog, a man named Fischer, eyed the black man in front of him with undisguised skepticism.

"This is the neighbor I was telling you about," Ramsey put in quickly. "I vouch for him."

Fischer scratched his belly and continued to stare at Leon for a moment. He frowned. "There could be another 3H outfit, you know. New Mexico. Texas. You just can't be sure that—"

"I'm sure," Ramsey said. "Mr. Brown's stock and mine range on the same public graze, Marshal. I'm familiar with his animals. I recognize most of those steers." He pointed to the ten head standing placidly in the confinement of the small pen. "That one, that one, those two over there, the three-year-old with the broken horn tip, that speckled one there. I can identify each of those animals as belonging to Mr. Brown, Marshal. I'll swear out an affidavit to that effect if you like."

The town marshal scratched his belly again and nodded. "I accept your word for that, Mr. Ramsey."

Leon felt sure the man wouldn't have accepted his word for the fact that the sun was shining.

At least Fischer seemed willing to be decent about it, though, now that Jud Ramsey swore to the validity of Leon's claim on the cattle.

And thank goodness that Ramsey did. On his own, Leon couldn't have sworn to such a claim. Aside from the fact that he still had seen only a very few of the cattle that were supposed to be his, Leon wouldn't have been able to recognize one cow from another.

It was different with horses, of course. Horses a man

simply knew. But not cows. Or at least Leon could not yet see them as individuals. He simply didn't have the familiarity with cows that he did with horses. There was no way he could have sworn in a court of law—if it came to that—that these particular cows with the 3H brand were his particular cows.

Marshal Fischer sighed heavily. He looked like a man having acute gas pains in his belly.

"While I was waiting for you to get here, Mr. Ramsey, I had a word with Mr. Hitchins. And with the boys Hitchins bought those steers off of."

Ramsey raised an eyebrow. Leon remained quiet. The marshal seemed comfortable enough talking to Ramsey about it. Leon didn't want to muddy the waters if he didn't have to. It was enough asking the local law to do something. Better not to rub Fischer's nose in the fact that a black man was making a claim against a white.

"I have to tell you, Mr. Ramsey, that the young men are from Kazumal. That, uh, seems to support the claim by, uh, Brown here."

Leon averted his eyes from Fischer. He'd done it for so long that it was a habit now, so ingrained it hardly even seemed demeaning. Although it was.

"The boys swear to me that they thought the cattle were strays. They, uh, say they were going to post the sale in the county brand book and pay the proceeds to the owner, except o' course for the usual dollar a head."

Leon had heard of that custom in Texas, although there it was said to be long outmoded, a carryover from the war days when Texas cattle ran virtually wild and anyone was free to clear his range of stray stock by selling the animals, keeping one dollar for himself and sending the rest on to whoever owned the branded livestock.

Here, Leon guessed, the procedure was an excuse rather than a practice.

Ramsey voiced what Leon could not.

"Bullshit," the neighbor said firmly.

"I'm only saying what they told me, Mr. Ramsey."

"And I'm only saying what I think of their statement, Marshal Fischer. It is bullshit, sir."

"Yes, well, uh, what I think I should do here is collect Brown's money from those young men." For the first time he looked directly at Leon and not at Ramsey. "I will collect all of it. No dollar holdback."

"You should charge them with—"

"Leave it be, Mr. Ramsey," Fischer said in a soft voice. "I think it would be best to just leave it be. I'll collect Brown's money. And I'll make sure the handlers at the pens here know that the 3H is a valid brand in Comas County. This won't happen again."

"But—"

"Thank you, Marshal. Thank you kindly," Leon said quickly.

Recovery of the sale money and warning off the thieves were really more than Leon could have expected. Certainly more than he would have gotten in Kazumal.

Fischer nodded. Out of the corner of his eye he gave Leon a glance that was almost grateful. The man was doing what he had to but he didn't want to antagonize white men in favor of a Negro. Leon understood the problem and appreciated the marshal's willingness to go this far.

Jud Ramsey did not, apparently.

"Marshal, I still think you ought to—"

"Mr. Ramsey. Please don't," Leon said.

Ramsey grunted and grumped but he let it go, asking instead, "You say the people in question are young men, Marshal?"

Fischer nodded again. "You probably know them." He hesitated. "A couple brothers name of Tucker."

From the way the man said it, Leon got the impression that the people of Douglas and perhaps Marshal Fischer in particular knew the Tucker family also. And not necessarily with favor.

"Those little—"

"Thank you, Marshal Fischer," Leon cut Ramsey off. "You've been real helpful."

Fischer grunted. He accepted Ramsey's thanks with more enthusiasm.

"I'll collect the money this afternoon," Fischer said.

"Where will you be, Brown?" The man was unable to tack a "mister" in front of the name, but at least he was making an attempt to be civil. Leon appreciated that too.

"I'll want to do some shopping in your town, Marshal, but I could come back here later tonight and wait for you." There likely wouldn't be a hotel in Douglas that would accept a black guest. Leon figured to sleep tonight by the pens and get an early start tomorrow morning. Jud Ramsey had already said he intended to stay on in Douglas for a few more days.

"That'll be fine." Fischer shook hands with Ramsey, nodded to Leon and walked off in the direction of the business district.

"Those sorry little sons of—"

"It's all right, Mr. Ramsey. Truly it is." Leon smiled. "Worked out a whole lot better than I could've expected, thanks to you."

Ramsey grunted.

'The point is, it's taken care of now. Thank you for that."

Ramsey shrugged. "I'll let it go, then, if you like." He brightened a little. "I still have to collect for these beefs. And you haven't told me yet if you're satisfied with the deal I found for your horses."

Leon grinned. "Mr. Ramsey, I got to tell you, what with selling the horses and getting money for those steers too, why, I'm gonna have more money in my pocket tonight than I guess I've ever seen all at one time before now. It practically makes me feel like a rich man, and I got to thank you for that too."

"Huh! You're the one did all the work, Mr. Brown. No credit to me for it."

For some reason Ramsey seemed almost grumpy again.

"Well, I thank you anyway, Mr. Ramsey."

"Huh." He fidgeted for a moment, then said, "Come along, Mr. Brown. You'll want to meet the man who's buying those 3H geldings and collect your pay for them."

"Yes, indeed, Mr. Ramsey, I surely will."

17

Leon felt like a rich man indeed when he crawled under his blanket that evening.

The eleven geldings brought twenty-two dollars per head. The cattle the Tuckers tried to steal from him had sold for an incredible thirty-four dollars each.

Leon couldn't help grinning and touching his money belt now and then. There was nearly six hundred dollars in the belt, including the few he'd brought with him from home.

Anne May was going to be proud, he thought.

For that matter, he was proud of the accomplishment himself. Just today he had earned $582 for a single summer's work.

In the army, even at a corporal's rate of pay, it would have taken him . . . Why, he couldn't hardly work out how long it would take for a corporal to make that much money. Three years? Something like that.

He grinned just from thinking about it. Three years pay in a single afternoon. The idea was overwhelming.

He lay with his head on the seat of the saddle Jud Ramsey had given him—no, dammit, Ramsey had not given him the saddle; he had damned well earned it helping the man drive his cows here—and stared happily toward the distant stars.

Arizona was a land of boundless opportunity. Even for a man whose skin was dark.

The only thing Leon needed now was for Anne May to join him. And that could only be a matter of days now.

By the time he got home her letter would be waiting

for him at the post office. Or she might even be waiting for him at the ranch by the time he got there.

Her letter could've gotten lost somehow. Anne May might be on a coach to Kazumal right this very minute.

Leon wriggled with pleased anticipation just at the thought.

He wanted to sleep. He wanted to be rested for tomorrow's start for home. The truth was that he was too excited from thinking about Anne May to sleep now.

He lay wide awake and completely happy, thinking about how fine the reunion would be when Anne May got here.

No man could want any more from life than Leon Brown had at this moment.

18

My oh my, now wasn't this interesting. Leon lay rigid under his blanket with his eyes wide open.

Someone was creeping around in the night not so very far away.

He could hear the soft, grinding crunch of the fellow's footsteps moving slow over the gravel-sprinkled soil.

The one and—he wasn't so sure about it—the quieter sounds of a second person moving behind the first one.

He cocked his head to the side and listened more closely for a moment, then nodded to himself.

Two of them. And they were sure trying to put the sneak on.

Dumb bastards, he thought. He had been snuck up on by better men than them.

He had been snuck up on by Apache and Kiowa and Comanche, and those fellows were a whole lot better at it than these ones were.

Leon smiled quietly toward the stars.

Even a wool-headed nigger—which these boys undoubtedly thought he was—has to learn a few things if he wants to keep his woolly hair when he's out playing with the fellas who really know how to put on a sneak.

Why, if the dumb SOBs had just walked up to him loud and normal he likely wouldn't have thought a thing about it. Just some fellows walking along in the night.

But when they went creeping along on tippy-toe and almost quiet, that sure drew a fellow's attention.

Leon might have felt sorry for the dummies except that they were probably after the near six hundred dollars he

had in his belt. That amount of money was serious enough
that he couldn't work up much of a sorry feeling.

He did hope, though, that he wasn't going to have to
hurt anybody over this. That was just about the last thing
he needed: Marshal Fischer coming around now to ask
why Leon had gone and shot a white man or two in the
marshal's quiet town.

Leon grimaced. With any kind of luck maybe these
two fellows would turn out to be Mexicans. The marshal
would probably look kinder on him if he shot a Mexican
rather than a white man.

He exhaled loudly and turned onto his side as if shifting positions in his sleep. Out in the darkness the cautious footsteps halted for a moment, waiting for Leon to
return to the deep sleep they would be thinking he was
in.

Instead, he snaked a hand up under the cover of the
blanket and reached underneath the tree of the old saddle
he had gotten from Jud Ramsey. His holstered army Colt
was there, the belt wrapped around it. He slid the gun
free and back down under the blanket.

Somebody was fixing to be in for a surprise.

Leon tensed as the surreptitious footsteps came together, and the two men stopped about thirty, forty yards
away.

They would be whispering about it, he figured. Plan-
ning who was going to do what and when.

The real question was, what was he going to do about
it, damn them.

Scare them off, he decided.

It was better to do that than risk spending time in Marshal Fischer's jail, blast their hides.

He waited, the silence oppressive now.

If they shot from right where they were, he might have
no warning. What he needed was for them . . .

His mouth stretched in a thin smile when he heard the
soft, cautious approach of one set of footsteps.

One of them was hanging back to provide cover while
the other crept in for a close shot.

That was all right. Leon could handle that just fine, thank you.

Seven yards, he figured. The guy would want to be within about seven yards. For some reason—he didn't pretend to understand it, but he knew that it was true enough to count on—seven yards was just about the place where nearly anyone felt comfortable shooting.

Unless the guy had a shotgun. A man tended to feel more confident with a shotgun and might try from farther away if that was what he was carrying.

Leon put the thought away. Not that many men in this country carried shotguns. It was mostly revolvers and some rifles or carbines. Probably the fellow had a revolver. He could walk the streets that way and not stand out in the crowd after the excitement of the shooting.

The footsteps were within twenty yards now. Fifteen. Ten.

Leon tensed and prepared himself under the blanket. He knew just what he was going to have to do. He didn't like it particularly, but he was ready.

The footsteps stopped.

For a moment there was no sound at all.

Then Leon could hear the metallic *clack* of a gun hammer being cocked.

The silly SOB hadn't even come in with his revolver ready. And judging from how loud the sounds were as the hammer stop engaged the sear first at half-cock and then at the let-'er-rip detent, the guy hadn't even sense enough to muffle the noise against his belly.

Dumb, Leon thought.

Even as he thought it he was moving.

He rolled violently to the side, taking the blanket with him and sending the saddle flying.

"Hey!"

His shout boomed out loud in the night, startling the would-be gunman probably as bad as the unexpected motion did.

From his position prone against the ground Leon could see the man silhouetted against the slightly lighter darkness of the starlit sky.

The man jumped a good foot into the air, and his finger tightened involuntarily against the trigger of the cocked revolver he was holding.

The gun exploded without aim, its bullet thumping into the ground somewhere between Leon and him.

Gravel sprayed from the spot where the bullet struck, and flame flicked bright and brief from the muzzle of the gun, lighting the short distance between them like a photographer's powder flash.

Leon fired back. His shot was quick but aimed with reasonable care.

Deliberately he blew it past the shooter's head.

Even as he fired he began to chuckle softly to himself. That slug would be passing close enough to the man's ear to sound like the world's biggest, nastiest son of a bitch of a hornet. It likely would be close enough to make the dummy wet his britches.

Leon heard something like a groan from the one who had come in close, and from behind him there was a yelp of surprise out of the other one.

Neither of the two hung around to talk about which of them was the more surprised to find the tables turned. Both of them whirled and took off at a high run toward downtown Douglas.

Leon could hear their boots pounding ground for a good minute, and he didn't doubt that the both of them were shaking and quaking over their narrow escape.

"Dumb sons of bitches," he mumbled softly to himself. He sat up and pulled the blanket off his shoulders, his hands moving from long habit to punch the empty cartridge casing out of the cylinder of the Colt and replace the spent round with a fresh one.

There had been the two loud gunshots close together. Apparently that wasn't enough to arouse excitement in Douglas. No one came to see what the shooting was all about.

That was just fine by Leon, though. He shoved the Colt back into his holster and stood to belt the rig around his hips.

He had no idea what time of night it was just now, but

he was certain that it was exactly the right time to get moving. No sense in hanging around and giving them a second try at him.

He picked up his saddle and blanket and carried them over to the pen where the old bitch mare was.

It wouldn't take him five minutes to be loaded and gone.

That should be just about enough, he thought.

19

Kazumal hadn't changed a whole lot while Leon was away. Somehow he had thought it would look different now—now that the town's most unwelcome citizen was a man of some financial substance.

He did feel good about that still. Almost good enough to consider putting his money into the bank. Except if he did that, they would only be looking for ways to get every penny out of him, and he needed what he had for his and Anne May's future.

He had stopped at home only long enough to hide most of the proceeds from the Douglas trip and switch his saddle to a fresh mare. The old bitch had worked hard enough on her way home. She didn't need the added aggravation of a trip to town too. And now, by golly, he had horses enough to give the tough old thing a rest.

Yessir, he had money in his pockets and livestock on his land and all the prospects in the world stretched out in front of him. Glaring sun and all, this was a fine day.

All he needed now to make everything complete was that letter from Anne May.

He stopped in front of the store that contained the post office and hitched the spotted red horse he'd been riding.

"Afternoon, Mr. Beamon. Any mail for me today?"

The postal clerk checked the general-delivery basket and shook his head. "Not today. Sorry."

Leon's face fell. "You're sure, Mr. Beamon?"

"I'm sorry. There isn't anything."

Leon sighed. "I sure was hoping . . ."

"Sorry."

"Yes, well, thanks for looking." Leon turned away from the window.

The day didn't seem as grand now as it had just a few moments before.

Still, there was a lot left to get ready before Anne May got here. He needed to buy some more groceries. Even coffee this time. He could afford it now. And he wanted to have some on hand in case Mr. Ramsey came to call again.

Maybe he should buy some cloth too. Anne May would likely want to put up some curtains at the windows once she got into her new home.

He smiled to himself. Of course she would! No point in him trying to make the curtains for her, of course. Making curtains wasn't exactly something a man learned from three hitches in the Tenth. But he could sure have the cloth on hand for when she arrived. That would please her.

And maybe a picture for the wall? He wondered what kind of picture would please her.

He looked around the store. The place carried just about everything, but drawings to hang on walls didn't seem to be a popular item in Kazumal—or at least not in this store.

He decided the picture could wait. Probably Anne May would want to pick something out for her own tastes anyhow. But the cloth he could get now and the groceries and maybe a bale of rope. A man never had enough rope on hand when he was working with livestock.

Another smile came over his face when he realized he could afford to go over to the smithy now and get a branding iron made up. W. T. Harrold likely had one, but the iron hadn't been left on the ranch—at least not that Leon could find.

It would really be something to have his own branding iron. Lordy, but it would.

"Something you need today?"

"What? Oh." Leon grinned sheepishly. "Guess I was stargazing. Yes, there's a number of things I need today."

"Got a list?"

"I came off in such a hurry, I didn't make one out."

Mr. Beamon, who was serving double duty today at both the post office and store counters, handed him a bit of paper and a pencil stub, and Leon spent several minutes marking down the items he wanted.

He handed the paper to Beamon finally and said, "It will take you a while to fill this. If you don't mind, I'll go on and take care of some other things and come back for the stuff later."

"Be ready when you are," Beamon agreed.

Now that Leon had thought about getting his own branding iron made, he could hardly wait to get the order in. He thanked the clerk and hurried out onto the street.

The blacksmith's shop was down beside the livery stable. Leon hoped the smith would be more agreeable than the hostler was. He left his mare where she was and walked down to the smithy.

The forge was hot when he got there, but there was no sign of the smith in the place.

"Hello? Is anybody here?"

Leon didn't want to enter the place if the proprietor wasn't around. That would be as good as asking for accusations. He stayed at the entrance and called out again, but there was no response.

The smith couldn't have gone far. Not with the forge so hot. Probably, Leon decided, he had gone out back for something.

Instead of walking through the building, Leon walked around the outside to a back yard that was littered with broken implements and scraps of iron.

"Hello?" He stopped well short of the junk that someone else might claim as valuable, and looked about. There was no sign of the town smith. "Hello?"

He certainly had been hoping to get that branding-iron order placed. It could wait if it had to, of course. It was just . . .

"What the hell are you bellowing about?"

The voice came from behind him. Leon turned. The hostler was standing there. What had Ramsey said the man's name was? Leon couldn't remember. Whoever he was, he wasn't alone. There were three men with him, all of them much younger. Leon thought he'd seen at least one of them here before. The three were all blond and belligerent. Part of the Tucker clan? Leon guessed that they might be even as he hoped they were not.

"I was looking for the blacksmith," Leon explained.

"You was disturbing the peace is what you was doing, standing back here shouting like that."

"I didn't mean to . . . I didn't mean to cause a commotion." Leon shifted from foot to foot nervously.

Damn these people anyway. All he wanted to do was to ask to have a branding iron made. There wasn't anything wrong with that.

"I'll come back some other time," he said.

"You stop where you are, nigger." It was one of the young men who said it. For some reason, for no reason, the man was getting red in the face.

He and his brothers or cousins or whoever the hell they were began edging closer, spreading out now, blocking Leon's path toward the front of the smithy.

They had no reason to do this, damn them.

No reason except that they were white and he wasn't. Apparently that was reason enough.

"I'll come back another time," Leon said patiently. "I'm sorry if I disturbed your peace."

None of the whites seemed to hear the sarcasm in his statement. They were too busy encircling him to listen.

The three younger men, the hostler hanging safely behind, jumped for him.

Leon first ducked a looping punch, blocked another with a quickly thrown forearm, and tried to back away.

He didn't want to get into a brawl with these three. Most of all he didn't want to hurt them.

He could, damn them. He could hurt them if he had to.

With a sick, sinking feeling in his gut he knew that hurting these three, even in clear self-defense, would only make things worse for him in Kazumal. Worse for him and, worst of all, worse for Anne May when she got here.

The best he could hope for would be to keep these three offays from hurting him.

He slapped a fist aside, tried to duck again, and recoiled as another blow came in from the side and caught him high on the side of the face.

He felt flesh tear and blood begin to flow.

"I don't . . ."

Something very solid smashed into the back of his head, and Leon felt himself fall.

He pitched forward, facedown in the dirt, and a floaty, distant, detached feeling came dreamily over him.

He could hear boots thump into his body and against his head, but oddly, pleasantly, he couldn't feel the impacts. He could only hear them.

"Damn," he mumbled. "I was only . . ."

He had time enough to hope that Anne May wouldn't arrive until he'd had a chance to heal some from this.

Then his time ran out, and he could hear and see and feel nothing at all anymore.

20

"Mr. Brown?"

Leon blinked. It was difficult to bring his vision into focus. It was blurry and red-tinged, and his entire body felt like someone had been beating on it with sticks. Well, probably someone had.

Lordy, he had never felt anything this bad before. He hadn't known it was possible to feel this bad and not be dead from it.

He tried to move, wanting to sit up, but that only made things worse. He winced and lay back, aware now that there was a pillow of some kind behind the back of his neck and that he was lying on a pallet under a roof somewhere.

"Don't try to move, Mr. Brown," the priest said.

Leon had to work for a moment to remember what the popist's name was. Father Felipe. It pleased him to be able to remember that.

"You've been hurt very badly, Mr. Brown. Please don't try to move."

It was probably good advice, but Leon ignored it. He struggled again to sit up, the effort of it tearing at his stomach and sending sharp, jabbing jolts of pain through his chest. At the very least he had some ribs broken. The question that was worrying him was whether there was any internal damage beyond that. It wasn't logical or reasonable, but he had a firm conviction that if he could just sit up, stand up, then everything would be all right again.

Father Felipe quit advising him and helped him instead, taking Leon's hands and helping to pull him into a sitting position.

A wave of dizziness made Leon's head swim and his vision blur again, but he felt better about being able to move.

His chest felt tight. He looked down and saw that his shirt was gone and the priest or someone else had bandaged his rib cage with strips of cotton cloth. The bandages were so tight it was difficult to breathe, but it was a good thing they were there. The wraps of cloth were probably all that was holding him together right now.

Leon tried to stand, but this time the priest was adamant. The old man placed a firm hand on his shoulder and wouldn't let him up.

"You are not in any shape for that, my son."

"Got to . . . I got to get up."

Father Felipe smiled gently and shook his head. "No. There is nothing you must do now but rest. Please."

Leon shuddered, the slight movement of it sending fresh fire bursts of pain through his upper body.

His head hurt, he noticed, but not as badly as he might have expected, and there were bone-deep pains in his arms and wrists and hands. He must have curled into a ball and tried to protect his head with his arms, although he didn't remember doing it.

"I have to get home. An' I got groceries to pick up at the store," he said stubbornly. He knew he was in no condition to walk, but he refused to admit it even to himself.

Father Felipe laughed. "You are a determined man, Mr. Brown. But then I suppose you would have to be, yes? Still, there is no point to this. The stores all closed hours ago. Some of my children found your horse. The red-spotted one, yes? A mare? She is being taken care of."

"Thanks." Leon squinted at the old priest. "I always thought you priests didn't have kids."

Father Felipe laughed again. "Not my own," he explained. "Children of my parish. Children of Jesus and Mary. My children only in the same way that you are my child, Mr. Brown."

"Oh." Leon wasn't entirely sure he liked being called

the child of a popist, but this didn't seem a good time to get into the subject. "Help me up, would you please? I got . . . got to get home anyway."

"Not tonight, Mr. Brown. Probably not for many days. It will be longer than you think before you can take care of yourself."

"Huh. Shorter than you think is what it'll be." He tried again to struggle to his feet, but the pain and the dizziness quickly drove him back down. Maybe the damn priest was right. Just for this minute, though. Just for right now. Another five, ten minutes. A half-hour at the most. Then Leon had to be moving. He had to get home. The old bitch mare was in the corral. She would be needing food and water. The thought of carrying water was terrible to imagine, but it would have to be done. At least one horse had to be kept in the pen if he wanted to maintain control over the rest of them. And leave them all alone for too long, and the whole damned herd would go right back to being as wild as they were the first day Leon saw them. He couldn't let that happen. He just couldn't.

The priest turned away for a moment. Leon could hear the dull chink of metal against metal. When Father Felipe turned back to him, there was a tin mug full of a steaming, aromatic beverage in the priest's hands.

"Drink this. It will soothe you."

"What is it?" Leon asked suspiciously. He'd never smelled anything quite like it before.

"Tea," Father Felipe said. "An herb tea. Very soothing. Very healing. Truly. I would not try to harm you."

Leon felt his cheeks flush with the quick heat of a blush. At least the priest would not likely notice it. Hell, his color was good for something besides getting him into trouble here. "I didn't mean . . . anything like that," he said quickly.

Leon tried to take the cup from the priest but discovered he was too weak and shaky to handle it. Father Felipe had to hold it to his lips and tilt it for him.

The tea, whatever was in it, had a heavy, smoky flavor, slightly bitter but oddly pleasant when the heat of it reached his stomach and spread through him.

"You say it's dark already?"

"Late. Very late." Father Felipe held the cup to Leon's mouth and made him drink again. "Finish it. Please. It will help you." He was still pouring the hot tea into Leon even as he spoke. Leon had a distinct choice in the matter. He could drink as the priest directed or he could choke. Considering the way his chest felt now and how much worse it would probably feel if he got to choking, he did the sensible thing and drank the tea.

"Good. Thank you," the priest said.

"I guess . . . I'm the one should be thanking you."

Father Felipe smiled. "The time for that will come." The smile got wider. "In God's time, yes?" Father Felipe took him gently by the shoulders and eased him back down onto the pallet. "Sleep now. Rest and heal."

Leon knew he should protest. He should get right up from here and start for home. But, Lordy, he was awful sleepy all of a sudden. His eyelids kept dragging closed no matter how hard he blinked and struggled, and he could feel himself sliding off into the sleep the priest wanted him in.

Damn fellow had given him something in that tea to make him sleep whether he wanted to or not, Leon decided.

Too late to think about it now, though.

It was the last thought Leon had for some time.

21

In the morning, incredibly, he hurt even worse than he had just after the damage was done. All the aches and pains seemed to have been driven deep into his bones while he slept, and his chest hurt so badly it was almost impossible to breathe, bandages or no.

Father Felipe brought him a breakfast of weak tea—without anything in it to help him sleep, the priest swore—and some odd, flat, cornmeal concoctions smeared with a mushlike bean mixture. The food was strange but also welcome.

"I need to get up now," Leon announced after he ate.

Father Felipe shook his head. "That would not be wise, my son."

Leon felt his cheeks heat again. "Look, uh, Father, it's kinda necessary. I have to, you know, go out back."

The priest smiled and shook his head. "Stay here. I will bring you something."

He did, but it was damned embarrassing. Leon had never needed help with that particular function in his life, and he didn't like needing it now.

"Lie still," Father Felipe told him. The advice was unnecessary. Leon wasn't going anywhere without assistance.

The priest left. He returned several minutes later with a dark-skinned woman who was wearing Mexican clothing. It took Leon a minute to recognize her as the same woman he and the priest had found beaten in that alley. She would never be anything close to attractive, but she certainly looked better now than she had that night.

Leon groped to remember the half-Mexican/half-Apache woman's name, but it wouldn't come to him.

"Manuela heard about your injuries," Father Felipe said helpfully. And quickly enough that Leon wondered if the priest recognized his problem and was trying to do something about it without being obvious. "She asked if she could repay your kindness by tending to you while you are ill."

Leon turned his head away. "I . . . No need for that. I can manage."

"I wish that was true, my son, but it is not." He gently prodded Manuela on into the room.

"Please, señor? It would please me."

Had he heard Manuela speak before? He couldn't remember. She had a nice voice, though. Very soft and very kind. Her eyes were large and soft as well now that they weren't wracked with pain.

"I don't need to be a bother to anybody," Leon insisted. "Really. I'll just rest here a few more minutes an' get for home. I'll be fine."

"You will not," Manuela said firmly before Father Felipe could speak up. "I will take care of you. I insist."

"No. Really . . ." Leon's protests were totally in vain.

Even while he was telling them not to, Father Felipe and Manuela set about bathing him and dressing his cuts with some evil-smelling salve.

Leon thought he'd never been so damned embarrassed in his life. He was sure he hadn't. The idea that a woman should see him, bathe him . . .

Nothing he said had any effect on either Manuela or the priest, though, and when it came right down to it, he was incapable of doing anything to stop them.

"Dammit," Leon moaned, "I got to get home. I've got a horse in the corral that'll die if I'm not there to tend it. And . . . and other stuff."

"I will take care of it," Manuela said lightly, continuing to wash him from a small basin of warm water as if it were the most natural thing possible.

"Later," Father Felipe said. "This afternoon, maybe,

I will find a cart to take you and Manuela to your ranch.'' He smiled. "Don't worry. She will take care of everything."

"I don't have any money to pay her with," Leon said. It wasn't really true, but he was grasping at straws. Not that it seemed to matter what he said or did or wanted. The priest continued to smile, and Manuela continued to wash, and Leon continued to suffer.

"You are blushing," Manuela said at one point. "There is no need for that, Señor Brown." She put her washrag aside and began using a tattered scrap of towel to dry him.

Leon looked at her closely. She didn't seem to notice.

The strange thing about that comment, the really strange thing, was that Manuela had been able to see that he was blushing. She had quite a lot of him to see, of course. But even so. No non-Negro ever noticed a black man blush—at least not that Leon knew about. This one did, though. Odd, he thought.

He closed his eyes and tried to pretend that none of this was happening to him. Not the beating, not the pain, not the priest, and certainly not this woman who was handling him like no female except his mother ever had. And hadn't that been a very long time ago?

"This afternoon," Leon insisted. "I got to go home this afternoon."

"As God wills," the priest said calmly.

Manuela just kept on with what she was doing.

22

Leon had no idea when they reached the house. He passed out shortly after the two-wheeled *carreta* jolted out of Kazumal. When he came to again, the Mexicans who had been helping were already gone and Manuela was at the stove stirring a pot with a marvelous soup smell coming out of it.

She stopped what she was doing and came to his side when Leon groaned.

"Lie still." She took a bit of rag from a pocket on her skirt and used it to wipe his forehead. He hadn't realized how he was sweating until she did that. Then, realizing, he began to shiver.

"I think the bumping made it worse," she said.

Judging from the way he felt now, Leon had to agree with her. Maybe it had been a mistake making Father Felipe send him back to the ranch. His chest and lower torso felt like everything inside him had been ripped out and crudely stuffed back where it belonged. He coughed, and that sent arrows of pain through him. Better not to cough again, he decided.

Manuela wiped his forehead some more. "Rest now."

"The horse. . . ." It hurt to talk too, although not as badly as the coughing did.

"I already saw to it. And the one you had in town."

Leon couldn't remember them bringing the horse along. But then he couldn't remember very much about the trip from Kazumal to home. It was probably just as well that he didn't. He nodded and hoped Manuela understood the gesture as a thank you.

"Rest now," Manuela said again. "When you wake, you can eat. Then sleep again, eh?"

His eyes dragged closed and he tried to let his body go loose and limp. Tightening up against pain was the worst thing you could do. If you could go loose, completely and absolutely loose, the body would float away from the mind where the pain was held, and the pain wouldn't be so bad. A gray-haired old private first class, a man whose past owners had not always been considerate, taught Leon that a very long time ago and the advice had been proven sound.

A smile lay forgotten on his lips, and Leon thought he heard himself begin to snore.

23

The Indian rose up out of the mist.

The Indian's face was painted. Hideous. A fright mask. A death mask.

The Indian's face was chalky white on one side and stark empty black on the other.

His hair was braided and ropy with grease.

He had a brass tomahawk raised in one fist, the blade of it glinting gold in the murky light, and a vermilion war club in the other.

His mouth was open, and Leon knew the Indian was shrieking his rage and hatred although both of them moved in ghostlike silence.

Leon tired to lift his carbine. The Springfield was heavy, as if made of lead, and Leon's arms were weak. He jerked its trigger again and again. There was no sound, no burst of smoke from the muzzle. No solid, satisfying feel of recoil.

He looked down. The Springfield's hammer had rusted and fallen away. The hinged breechblock was gone.

The Indian was still coming. He was closer now, his eyes wide and dark and empty of life like deep, hollow pits.

The tomahawk flashed over his head.

The Indian was huge. He loomed above Leon's frozen stare. Sweat and grease glistened on his massive arms and torso.

The blade of the tomahawk descended.

Leon heard a scream and distantly knew that it was his own.

He tried to run and from nowhere pain shot through his body.

His eyes snapped open as he came out of the nightmare, and he screamed a second time as the dream vision seemed to follow him even into wakefulness.

He was confronted by huge, dark eyes only inches in front of his face. The scream choked short in his throat as awareness reached him.

The eyes were Manuela's. They were as large and as black as the dream warrior's had been. But in these there were compassion and concern. These eyes were warm and alive and glistening, not the dull, empty things of the dream warrior.

"Shhh, shhh, shhh now." Manuela took up a cloth and ran it gently over his forehead.

Leon relaxed back against the bed. He was trembling and covered with chill sweat.

"You were asleep. You yelled. You were afraid, but it is right now. I am here with you."

She smiled, the tug of it making deep crow's-feet at the corners of her eyes. Leon could feel her hand find his and squeeze lightly, assuring him of her presence.

He nodded, unsure if he could speak for the moment. There was still a sharp aftermath of pain in his chest from the involuntary movement he'd made when he tried to run away from the warrior in the dream.

It must have been that, just the pain, that caused him to cry out, he believed.

Manuela wiped his face and ran her hand over his forehead and down, forcing his eyes closed again.

"It will all be well," she promised.

A sob caught in Leon's chest. But after a moment he was able to relax, and the healing sleep reached up to claim him again.

The last thing he remembered was a soft, crooning song that Manuela was humming to him.

24

Leon smiled. "You're a good cook."

"Thank you." Manuela looked away from him as if she were embarrassed by the comment.

He lifted a fragment of meat to his mouth and chewed slowly. She had cut it up into tiny bits for him so he wouldn't have to struggle with it, but the flavor was wonderful. "What is it?"

"Deer."

"How'd you get deer meat?"

"Shoot it."

"Shoot it? What with?"

She pointed toward a corner. A long-barreled, two-band infantry-model trapdoor Springfield stood there now. Leon had never seen the rifle before. It certainly was not his.

"A man brought it. Said was yours."

It took Leon a moment to figure out who might have brought a rifle and claimed it was his. "Mr. Ramsey was here?"

Manuela nodded. "Ramsey, yes."

"And he didn't come in?"

She laughed. "Came in. Sat with you a time. You were asleep."

"When the devil was all this?"

She had to think about that for a moment. "Three days? Four could be. No, three. Yesterday I shoot the deer. Day before that Ramsey he come."

Leon shook his head. "How long . . . ?"

Manuela shrugged. "Week could be."

"Damn." He realized what he'd said and blushed. "I'm sorry ma'am. That just slipped out."

Manuela gave him an odd look, then nodded solemnly. "Thank you."

He took another bite of the fresh venison. Even knowing what it was, he could hardly believe the excellent meat was deer. Leon's past experience with venison was that the stuff was dry, stringy, and barely palatable. But that had always been soldier's cooking. Somehow Manuela had made the nearly fatless meat juicy and tender and marvelously strength-giving.

"Yes, ma'am, you're a fine cook."

Manuela ducked her head nervously.

25

Leon groaned and faced the wall until he heard Manuela's footsteps receding around the outside of the house and on toward the back.

This was the most uncomfortable thing of all, the fact that she had to tend to his bodily functions. He'd argued with her this morning. Insisted that she help him upright so he could at least do that small thing for himself. It was no good. He hadn't been able to manage it and nearly passed out from the intense pain of trying.

Dammit, though, it made him feel like a helpless, useless babe.

Manuela returned and set the bucket aside. Leon wouldn't look at her.

She ignored his obvious discomfort and brought a dishpan of soapy water that she used quite matter-of-factly to wash him.

"Señor Brown."

"Yes?" He continued to stare at the wall beside his bed.

"You are a good man, Señor Brown. You should not worry so about things of no importance." She raised his left arm gently and washed his armpit, then rinsed and quickly dried it. He heard a low, soft chuckle. "You should not blush so, neither."

Leon rolled his head so he could see her. She was smiling and didn't seem embarrassed in the slightest. He looked away again.

"I have a favor to ask, Señor Brown."

"Of course. Whatever you like."

"It is Saturday. Tonight I should like to go to town. Be back tomorrow morning as early as I can."

The thought of trying to cope alone in the small house without her brought a clenching in his gut. He was weak and helpless and entirely useless. But he certainly had no right to make claims on this poor woman. It was Saturday night and of course she would be needing to go to town. Hell, she had her own life to live, hard as it might be. And much as he might resent it right now.

He nodded, his expression impassive. A blank, empty window for the world to see was an expression he had cultivated long, long ago and was never likely to forget. "Of course, ma'am."

"I will make you comfortable before I go." She continued to wash him, talking as she worked. "I will put food and water where you can reach and a pan for the other needs. The horses I will tend. You must not worry. I will be back tomorrow." She used a towel to pat dry his chest and stomach very carefully so she wouldn't cause him any pain.

"You don't have to. I can manage."

Her answering smile was a trifle grim. "You know better. So do I."

It was the simple truth, of course. He couldn't manage, dammit.

Those offays had done too good a job on him. They had come closer than Leon had thought to killing him.

And they wouldn't have cared if they did.

Just about the only person in the whole world who would care was Anne May, and she was a thousand miles away.

A thought struck him and he stiffened, bringing pain.

Manuela noticed. Quickly she dropped her washcloth and reached out to soothe him with a gentle palm on his forehead. "It is bad now?"

Leon didn't answer. He was thinking about Anne May. She might be on her way to Kazumal at this very moment. At the very least her letter should be waiting for him by now.

"Would you . . . would it be possible for you to check the mail while you're in town?" he asked.

"I don' know. I have never had mail myself, hmm. I don't know how to do this."

He explained it to her.

Manuela reflected for a moment, then said, "I can do, but I must go before dark. The store will close too soon if I wait."

"It . . . isn't important."

"Now you tell me a lie, Señor Brown." She resumed washing him now that the pain had subsided and his body was loose and relaxed again. "It is a thing of great importance to you. I see it in your face." She was smiling again. Encouraging him.

Leon didn't mean to. He really didn't. But he found himself telling Manuela about Anne May. What a wonderful woman Anne May was. How patient Anne May was with him.

"Fifteen years I was in the army," Leon said. "I'd met Anne May just before I enlisted the first time. She was a big part of the reason I did enlist, I guess. I mean, there wasn't any future for a nigger boy in Kansas City."

Manuela interrupted him. "You should not talk so. I know, I am called many things too. I do not call myself those things, hmm?"

Leon tried to shrug, found the resistance of pain in his torn muscles, and gave it up. "Whatever," he said. "Anyway, I had it in mind that I could make something of myself. For Anne May. So I enlisted. An' when the chaplain held classes—that was part of his job, I guess, but I'm sure grateful to the man for how well he did it— I went to all of them. Learned to read and write and figure. Learned to talk better. Learned a lot of things. Things the whites would've thought I was too dumb to learn. But I did. For Anne May." He sighed.

"She was the one thought I should make a career of it. I was only one hitch short. But I'd been saving my money and doing whatever I could to make extra, and then . . . Well, something happened that I got kinda down on the army. Kinda discouraged. But by then I had enough to buy this place." He smiled. "It's mine, you know. Free and clear and not a penny owing. Or I should say mine an' Anne May's, because as quick as she gets here we'll be married, and it'll belong to the both of us."

"I am happy for you, Señor Brown." She began washing him again. "Land of your own is a wonderful thing. A truly wonderful thing. This lady of yours must be very happy too."

Leon smiled. "I hope so. That's why I want you to call for the mail. To see if there's a letter saying when she'll be here."

"I will do it. You will have to have your supper early, hmm? So I can go to the store before it is closed. I don' know for sure when the gringo stores close, but I will leave you early and be there in time. If you have mail I will bring it." Her hands stopped moving, and she frowned. "If they will give it to me."

Leon hadn't thought about that. Manuela was about as much of an outcast in Kazumal as he was. Neither of them could expect much in the way of favors.

"I'll write out a note," he said. "I'll authorize them to give it to you. If there's any problem about it, I suppose you could ask the priest to help."

Manuela nodded but didn't look pleased.

"You aren't much in the habit of asking for favors either, are you?" he guessed. It pleased him now to realize that she'd said she wanted to ask a favor when she told him she wanted to go to town. It meant she wasn't frightened of him, maybe even was comfortable with him, despite his different color.

She shook her head. "You write out the note. Maybe I don' have to ask."

"You'll have to bring me the paper and my writing stuff."

"You tell me where."

Later, when the bath was mercifully over and she brought the paper and ink and pens to him, Manuela handled the materials with something approaching awe. Almost as if they were holy things. And she treated the note he wrote with reverence when she folded it with exceptional care and placed it inside her loose blouse for safe-keeping.

Leon suspected that Manuela didn't know how to read. He thought about offering to teach her—he certainly had nothing better to do with his time while he was laid up—but didn't know if the suggestion would offend her.

He settled for doing nothing for the time being.

Before she left, Manuela cooked a good meal for him—there was certainly something to be said for having a decent cook in the house—and did the dishes and some unnecessary housekeeping. She placed his makeshift bed-pan beside him and pulled a chair within arm's reach so he could help himself to water and cold food while she was away.

"I'll be fine," he assured her.

Manuela hesitated in the doorway for a moment, then disappeared.

Leon squeezed his eyes closed. In spite of the assurances, Manuela's and his own, he felt very much alone once she was gone. It was a feeling he couldn't remember ever having before.

26

It was already well past daylight before Leon heard the approach of footsteps outside the door.

He began to smile, thinking Manuela was back. Then the smile froze in place and a thrill of fear shot though him as he realized he could hear the soft chime of spur rowels as the footsteps came nearer.

If it was those men . . . come to finish what they started . . . come to burn him out maybe . . .

He tried to struggle into a sitting position.

The rifle was all the way across the room in the corner. He had no idea where his Colt had gotten to. He should have thought to ask Manuela to give him the revolver, at least.

He was not going die lying flat on his back in a damned sickbed.

He just would not.

He grabbed the side of the bed and tried to pull himself up, levering frantically with his elbow and other arm.

The pain tore at him and he cried out. But he didn't stop trying to get up.

The footsteps quickened.

Jud Ramsey ran in, a worried look on him.

"Jesus. It's you." Leon fell back against the bed. He was sweating again and the pain was excruciating.

"Are you all right, Mr. Brown?"

"I thought . . ." Leon shook his head. "It was nothing."

Ramsey looked around. "The little slut from town. She left? You should have told her to get word to me."

"She just had to go to town for a little while," Leon

explained. "She'll be back soon." He found himself resenting the fact that Mr. Ramsey called Manuela a slut.
She was, he supposed. A slut, a *puta,* a whore, whatever
Ramsey or anyone else wanted to call her. That was the
way she made her lousy living. But dammit . . .

Ramsey nodded. "Can I get you anything?" He removed his hat and stood awkwardly in the doorway.

Leon shook his head. "Thanks. She fixed me up fine
before she left." He motioned toward the plate of cold
meat and tortillas and the water jar. He smiled. "I'd offer
to get you something, Mr. Ramsey, but, uh . . ."

Ramsey smiled and seemed to relax.

"Help yourself, Mr. Ramsey. I, uh, never had time to
pick up my order at the store, so I can't offer you coffee.
But Manuela brought in some herbs that she's been making tea from. You could brew some of that for yourself."

"Would you like some?"

"Sure."

Ramsey dropped his hat on the table and began building a fire in the stove.

"The herbs are in that tin box. No, that one. That's
right."

Ramsey looked inside the container, shrugged, and
dumped a healthy quantity of the dried leaves into a pot.

"I want to thank you for the rifle, Mr. Ramsey. That
was kind of you."

"Just neighborly." He poured water from the bucket
into the pot and set it on the stove. The fire was beginning to draw now, bright flame flickering behind the stove
door and the gusty hum of its wind vibrating from the
stovepipe.

"Was there something special that brought you here,
Mr. Ramsey?"

"Not really." Ramsey smiled. "It's a Sunday morning. Visiting day. I just thought I'd see how you're getting along."

"Just wonderful well," Leon said dryly.

"So I see." Ramsey's voice was just as dry.

"I'm on the mend, though. I won't be down long."

"Good." Ramsey smiled again. "Something I wanted

to mention while I was here, Mr. Brown, that wild stud horse you turned loose?''

Leon nodded.

''The son of a buck's found himself a new harem. I spotted them when I was riding near the spring south of here. Went out to check my cattle and jumped a bunch of mustangs with that stallion. No idea where he found them or what he had to do to claim them, but he has a pretty nice bunch with him again.''

''Sure didn't take him long.''

''Really. I'd like to have seen the fight when he took them away from the other stud. Anyway, I thought you might want to know.''

''They aren't branded?''

''Not that I could see, and I was pretty close. I'm sure they're wild ones.''

''And you aren't interested in them?''

Ramsey laughed. ''Mr. Brown, when a man gets to my age, with his bones turning brittle, mustangs are something he resents and wants off his range. They sure aren't something he wants to go chasing after himself. Mustanging is a young man's game. No, if I was going to do anything about them at all, I might shoot them. But I sure wouldn't try to trap and break them like you did with that first bunch.''

''I thank you for the suggestion, Mr. Ramsey.''

The neighbor hesitated for a moment before he spoke again. ''You've got a tough-enough road in front of you if you want to make it here, Mr. Brown. I guess I just don't want to see it be any worse than it has to be.'' Ramsey cleared his throat and then smiled. ''Did your letter get here?''

Leon grinned. ''That's what I'm fixing to find out when Manuela gets back. I surely do hope so.''

27

Manuela was shy when she returned and found Jud Ramsey seated at the table. She seemed unwilling to meet the white man's eyes and retreated quickly to a corner where she was out of the way.

Ramsey, for his part, largely ignored Manuela too.

"Did you get the mail?" Leon asked.

"No mail." Her eyes remained down.

Disappointment clouded the moment for Leon. He'd been so sure . . .

He tried to look for a positive side to the information. He couldn't find one.

"Maybe tomorrow," Ramsey said helpfully. On the drive south to Douglas much of Leon's conversation had been about Anne May and the plans and hopes and dreams Leon had for the two of them. Ramsey understood the extent of Leon's disappointment.

"Sure," Leon said in a dull voice.

Ramsey slapped his thighs and stood. "I expect I should be getting on," he said a trifle too loudly. "Want to make a stop in town, then get on home before it comes dark."

Leon nodded but didn't look at him.

"Thanks for the tea."

Leon nodded again.

Ramsey put his hat on and left without a word to Manuela, nor had she spoken to him.

As soon as Ramsey was out the door, Manuela hurried to Leon's side. She laid the back of her wrist against his forehead and frowned but said nothing.

"Here," she said, reaching for the cut-down bucket that was his bedpan. "You need this."

Leon blushed furiously. But dammit, she was right. He did need it. He hadn't been able to ask a white gentleman like Mr. Ramsey to help him. Having Manuela do it was almost as bad.

"I will cook soon as you are clean, hmmm? Bet you are hungry, yes?"

Leon was too embarrassed even to speak. He faced the wall and tried to think about Anne May.

That evening, much later, he began to tremble with an onslaught of sudden chills.

Something in the aftermath of his injuries was bringing on a high fever. Manuela poured herbal teas into him and piled onto him all the blankets and bedding in the house, including the old bitch mare's horse blanket. Leon alternated between burning and freezing.

He wished Anne May was there to sit with him. He was not at all sure he would live to greet her if she delayed much longer.

28

Leon felt frail, as limp as cooked collards. He felt better, though—so much better now than he had in the past several weeks. He had come close to dying. Now he was very much on the mend.

For the first time since the Mexicans brought him home in their rattling *carreta* he was on his feet. Draped all over poor Manuela, of course, so that she was supporting fully half his weight. But he was upright for the very first time. That simple fact had come to mean a great deal to him.

Manuela helped him out into the bright glare of the Arizona sunlight. The light was burning on his eyes. And absolutely wonderful. He tipped his face up to it and closed his eyes, enjoying the heat and the brightness that came red and hard through his eyelids.

He was dizzy. Without Manuela's support he would have fallen. But he was walking. And best of all he was going to be able to go to the outhouse and tend to himself there. Manuela would have to help him make the trip. But once there, he could tend to himself.

A moment of acute embarrassment occurred when Manuela moved to his side and pulled Leon's arm over her shoulders.

He had been sick for a long time. But he'd been without a woman for much longer.

The feel of her warmth and the woman-softness of her body close against his brought an automatic and unwelcome male reaction.

Leon tried to ignore it. Tried to think about other things instead.

The fact that he had been thinking so very much about

Anne May these past weeks didn't help. Nor did the fact that Manuela's peasant blouse was distressingly loose at the neck. Whenever she bent over his bed these last few days he had been uncomfortably aware of her body beneath the thin cloth. At times she was much more fully revealed than he had any wish for her to be.

The sight of her, even so pale compared to his own dark flesh, was tantalizing. And frustrating.

He bit his underlip and tried to pretend that it was just another trooper helping him now. Guiding him the way you had to do when a man was grievously wounded and needed assistance to reach a travois on campaign.

The attempted self-deception didn't work at all.

Manuela was no black trooper helping out a buddy. She was a woman, soft and rounded and smelling nice.

Her hip was tight against his, and he was all too aware that his black-coffee-colored hand rested within inches of the soft bulge of the breast he'd seen so often when she didn't know the blouse was gaping.

"You are doing okay?"

He nodded. It was a lie. He was doing miserably. The weakness was only a small part of how poorly he was doing.

"Just a little more now. You want to rest?"

He wanted desperately to rest. He shook his head no. "I'll make it."

At least Manuela didn't seem to have noticed his predicament. There was that to be thankful for.

They reached the outhouse, and Manuela helped him inside.

"I leave you here. If you like, I can put the chair outside. The sun be good for you if you sit outside, mmm?"

Leon nodded. He felt infinitely grateful to be here now. And Lordy, it was good to be standing up on his own feet again.

He braced himself against the wall with both hands, and Manuela backed out of the tight quarters, closing the door behind her.

The privacy of the moment was almost as nice as the sunshine and fresh air had been.

29

Leon sat in the chair that had become his normal place of late. The late-afternoon sunlight was warm under the brim of his hat, warm through the thin cloth of his shirt. Even better, his belly felt warm and full. Earlier today Manuela had taken the old Springfield and gone out. She had brought back a wild desert bighorn. The animal was small, but its meat was tasty. A huge helping of fried chops rested now in Leon's stomach.

He heard Manuela come outside into the slanting light, and he turned his head.

She had freshened up after cooking. Her hair was still damp from being washed. She was smiling.

"All done. Dishes washed, everything clean. I put water for you an' more chops on the table if you get hungry again." She sounded slightly disbelieving that anyone could be hungry again within the next two weeks after putting away a meal like Leon just had.

"Is it Saturday night again?"

Manuela nodded. "Got to hurry or the store will close. Got to check the mail for you, mmm?"

He smiled. "Thank you."

Manuela shrugged.

"Isn't there something you want, Manuela? From the store, I mean?"

She shrugged again. "Could use some lard, maybe."

"I mean . . . like some new clothes or something. Lord knows, you're entitled. I have money. Why don't you get yourself something?" The clothes she was wearing now seemed to be all she owned.

"I don't need—"

"Please. It would make me feel better." She stead-fastly refused to take any pay for all the weeks of help she had given him, and he didn't believe he'd have sur-vived—literally wouldn't have survived his injuries and fevers—if it hadn't been for Manuela and her care. "A pretty blouse or a . . . I don't know, a nice dress?"

Manuela shrugged.

Leon took that to be acceptance. He dug in his pocket. He still had the money he had carried to town that day he was jumped. He'd never gotten around to spending any of it. And the cache of savings along with the profits from Douglas was still safe in the ground.

"Here." He gave her all of it, ten dollars, and Man-uela's eyes went wide.

"So much!"

"So little," he countered.

"I will get the lard and . . . some other things."

"And something nice for you," Leon insisted.

Manuela stood beside him and fussily made sure that his canes were where he could reach them and that the blanket was tucked tight around his legs. Leon was able to walk now with the support of the canes she had fash-ioned for him from wood scraps.

"I'll be just fine," he insisted.

"Of course you will." But she tidied and tucked any-way until she was satisfied that all was as it should be and that he would be all right until she returned.

Leon's mouth opened. He wanted to say something. What he really wanted to do was to ask Manuela to just go to town, check the mail, shop, and . . . come back again. She was much too good a woman to be spending her Saturday nights selling herself to the lower elements in Kazumal.

But it wasn't his right to tell her what to do, dammit.

Of all the people he had ever known—with the excep-tion of his mother and Anne May, of course—he owed Manuela more than anyone.

Simple understanding was a small-enough coin of re-payment.

He closed his mouth without speaking. Without complaining. Without forcing unwelcome advice on her.

"Thank you for checking the mail," he said again.

"De nada." She gave the lap robe a final, unnecessary tug and started off toward the little-used road to town.

"Where are you going?"

Manuela stopped and turned to give him a look like she suspected he had gone daft.

"I mean . . . you're walking?"

"Of course, Señor Brown. How else?"

"But . . ." Leon stammered, "there's a horse standing right there. It's eleven miles to town."

Manuela shrugged.

"You mean all this time you've been walking all the way to town and back?"

She shrugged again.

"Can't you ride a horse?"

"I think so."

Exasperated, Leon tried to struggle to his feet. Manuela ran back and stopped him from rising.

"Sit. You should rest. Please sit."

"I can saddle a horse for you, dammit."

She gave him an odd look. "I can do. If you are sure."

"Sure? Of course I'm sure."

She began to smile. "Be nice to not walk all the way."

"I should think so." He frowned. "All this time, all these Saturday nights, you've been walking?"

"What else?" Manuela seemed quite matter-of-fact about it, as if there was no other logical way to do things. Leon found the idea astounding. After all, he had made that walk himself. He knew how far and unpleasant it was.

"Don't you want me to help you saddle the horse?"

"You sit," she said quickly. "I will do."

He sat while Manuela inexpertly but with stubborn determination dragged out his saddle and bridle and put them on the old bitch mare.

"Be careful of that horse," Leon cautioned. "She's tough, but I won't claim she's mannerly."

The mare stood placid and calm, though, while Manuela climbed hand over hand up the stirrup leathers, clinging to the saddle horn for support until finally she was settled in the seat with her legs, much shorter than Leon's and unable to reach the stirrups where he had them, jutting out to the sides at an awkward angle.

Leon suspected the old bitch would have put him on his head if he ever tried to get onto her that way, but she didn't seem to mind Manuela's clumsiness in the slightest.

"You be careful," he warned again.

Manuela gave him a broad grin. She seemed pleased to be sitting on the tall horse and acted quite proud of herself now that she was there. She took her time about arranging the reins to her satisfaction—incorrectly, as a matter of fact, but the method she eventually came up with seemed to satisfy both Manuela and the old bitch mare well enough—then had to climb down again to open the gate. The mare stood rock-steady while Manuela did all that, and patiently allowed the woman to mount again.

"I be back early this time," Manuela said proudly. She thumped the mare in the sides with her bare heels, and the horse set out at a slow, gentle walk while Manuela sawed and pulled at the reins plow-fashion.

"Be damned," Leon muttered to himself. He tilted his head to let the sunlight strike the side of his face with its warmth and closed his eyes.

30

"You were in the army, no?"

"I was in the army, yes," Leon agreed. He bent closer to the cup, enjoying the steamy aroma of the fresh-brewed coffee. Manuela had brought coffee back from town for him—she didn't enjoy it, or so she said—and for herself only a hair ribbon to appease his instructions that she buy something. Stubborn damned woman. He did wish she'd buy a new blouse, though. The way this one flopped loose at the top was bothering him more and more. It seemed the harder he tried not to think about it, the more impossible it became.

"Long time?"

"Mmm." He nodded. "Three hitches. That's fifteen years. One more enlistment and I coulda retired."

"So? And you didn't stay?" She set more bowls on the table. Thick gravy and white rice. She bought the rice when she was in town too. She really was an excellent cook for having so little to work with.

Leon frowned and didn't answer.

Manuela finished putting Sunday dinner on the table and took a seat opposite him. Leon still found it strange that she'd be willing to sit at the same table with a black man, but the arrangement had held ever since he was strong enough to take his meals at the table and she seemed to think nothing of it.

He waited a moment before he dug into the bowls and plates of good food. By now he knew what to expect. Manuela quickly crossed herself and said something under her breath. When she looked up again, smiling, it was time to eat. He reached first for a slab of roast mutton.

"You don't say, but I think there was a good reason for you to leave. I see the pain in your eyes, Señor Brown."

Leon blinked. The depth of Manuela's perception was as disquieting as the fact that she took her meals with him. Or more so.

Not that he intended to tell her anything about it, of course. That would have been absolutely pointless. Absolutely pointless.

He opened his mouth, but instead of stuffing it with mutton, which he certainly should have done, he found himself telling her about it.

He'd intended to stay. He really had. It would have meant a retirement income for the rest of his life. And his savings would've been all that much more if he had stayed in for another hitch. Anne May wanted him to stay in and get the security of the retirement pay.

But . . . he just hadn't been able to.

He just got . . . discouraged.

He didn't want to stay after what they did to Lt. Flipper. He just didn't want to.

Manuela sat quiet and let him talk it out.

Leon had never told this to anyone before. Not even to Anne May, who'd been so bent on him remaining in uniform and taking the retirement.

Had never admitted to anyone just how—he didn't know exactly how to describe it—proud probably came closer than anything—of Lt. Flipper he had been.

All the officers were white men, Leon explained to her. And they were good officers for the most part. Not many of them seemed to look down on the men. And of course the troopers had long since worked things out with the white enlisted men so that one group pretty much left the other alone.

But there was one officer . . .

Lt. Henry Flipper was a black man. Just like Leon. He was black, and he was an officer. Commissioned by the

Congress of the United States. A black man and an officer.

It amazed Leon—and inspired him to, if the truth be known—to think about how very, very good Lt. Flipper must have been to get his rank.

Leon would've given anything he had, everything, just to be able to serve, just once, under Lt. Flipper.

Lt. Flipper was in the Ninth Cavalry, though. Leon was in the Tenth.

Once, just once, Leon saw Lt. Flipper. Didn't meet him exactly, enlisted men didn't meet officers, but he saw him. It was at Fort Gibson, over in Texas. Leon had contrived to walk past the lieutenant, just so he could snap a salute to the only black officer the army ever had. Maybe ever would have.

That—being able to salute Lt. Henry Flipper—was perhaps the proudest, most inspiring moment of Leon Brown's life.

It made him believe that if Lt. Henry Flipper could become an officer, Cpl. Leon Brown too could become anything he wanted if only he was willing to work hard enough at it.

Then Lt. Henry Flipper was cashiered. Kicked out of the army by white officers who resented a black man's excellence.

Leon believed that was what had happened. The rumors and tales among the men of the Ninth and the Tenth and in the black infantry regiments too were wild and mostly unbelievable. None of them knew for sure what the charges against Lt. Flipper were. Something about management of company funds. They knew that much. And they knew the real reason why Lt. Flipper was drummed out of the service. Lt. Flipper had gone horseback-riding once with a white woman, a relative of another officer at his post. That, Leon believed, was the real reason Lt. Flipper lost his commission.

It occurred to him while he was telling all of this to Manuela that she might not understand. She, after all, was no ''nigger'' woman. She was Mexican/Apache. She'd never had the experience of being a black human being in the white world. He kept talking, though. It was as if, once started, he couldn't stop. He sat at the table with Sunday dinner growing cold in front of him and poured it all out to silent, unquestioning Manuela.

Lt. Flipper was as close to being a living idol as Leon ever expected to have. He was good at what he did. And his "brother" officers saw to it that he was disgraced and cashiered.

If that could happen to Henry Flipper . . .

After that Leon had no real heart for the army. Anne May wanted him to stay in, but . . . he couldn't. He just couldn't do that. He had tried for a while. It just wasn't the same for him after Lt. Flipper was cashiered.

So, he tried to smile, here he was. The smile faltered, and there was a bleakness in his large brown eyes.

Manuela didn't speak. Instead, she leaned forward, reaching across the table, and squeezed his wrist with kindness and sympathy.

Leon blinked and turned his head away. After a moment he coughed and began to eat the now-cold meal. The two of them didn't speak again for some time.

31

"You're looking almost all right."

Leon grinned. "I'm feeling almost all right. Step down, Mr. Ramsey. This time I have some coffee to offer you."

"Why, I think I'll take you up on that, Mr. Brown." Ramsey dismounted and tied his horse to a rail at Leon's corral.

Manuela must have heard the conversation. She appeared in the doorway, a dish towel in her hands.

"Do we have any coffee, Manuela?"

"I put some on fresh." She darted away from the door.

"I'll be damned," Ramsey said. He stamped his boots and hitched his trousers. He must have been in the saddle for some time.

"What's that, Mr. Ramsey?"

"That Mex woman. She's still with you. I figured . . . Well, the truth is, I figured she was just here looking for a chance to pilfer something and take off on you. Never expected she'd stay and help like she's done."

"She's a good woman, Mr. Ramsey," Leon said with a calm intensity.

Ramsey grunted. "I didn't mean . . . I just know what she is. You know."

"I know what she's had to be, Mr. Ramsey. But she's really a good woman. Decent and kind and Christian. It's others, like those that beat me up, that've tried to make her something else."

"I never meant—"

"I'll tell you something else, Mr. Ramsey," Leon blurted. "If I could think of some way to keep her from having to go back to what she was, why, I'd sure do it. I surely would."

Leon had no idea where that came from. It was nothing he had consciously thought out beforehand. He hadn't had any notion of it before he heard himself telling it to Ramsey. It was, though, the way he honestly felt about it. There was no denying that.

"Sorry," Ramsey said. "All I know is what I hear in town."

"Sometimes people hear things that aren't so."

"True, Mr. Brown. Sadly true." Ramsey opened the near pocket on his saddlebags. "I found these in a drawer. Thought you might use them. I can't." He handed Leon a pasteboard box of .50-70 cartridges.

"Thank you, Mr. Ramsey."

"*De nada.* They were given to me. Now I've got no use for them. I suspect you do. I, uh, I've seen the woman there out hunting for meat. And I just thought you might need these."

"That's neighborly of you, Mr. Ramsey. Thank you." Leon smiled, and the slight awkwardness that had been in the air between them dissipated. "Come inside, Mr. Ramsey. That coffee will be ready soon. And Manuela made a rice pudding last night that's about as fine as anything a man could want to put a tooth to. I think this would be a good time to finish it before it spoils."

"I haven't had a rice pudding since my wife died, Mr. Brown." Ramsey smacked his hands together and grinned. "I would say you have just uncovered one of my weaknesses."

Leon motioned for Ramsey to go ahead, then followed him in. He needed only one cane now and wasn't relying on it very much anymore.

32

It was easier this time. Lordy, but it was easier.

It was coming dawn, and Leon could see the plume of dust just a quarter-mile away where the wild ones were running ahead of the roan mare. They were slowing. He eased back on the roan's rein. It was too soon to really push them.

They passed the pale, rocky hillock for . . . He could not remember how many times they had been past it by now. Five miles ahead and the wild band would swing wide around the camp where Manuela was waiting. Manuela and the old bitch mare. They would take up the chase from there.

That was something Leon hadn't expected. Manuela insisted. She actually enjoyed the riding, or so she said.

So she and the bitch mare relieved him for a swing around the wild herd's circle while he rested, then he and another horse would pick it up again.

Two and a half days and nights they had been going like this, and already the circles were becoming shorter and the wild horses slower.

It was going to be over quicker this time, Leon thought. Not so much because this group of wild horses was in poorer condition than the others had been, but because the stallion didn't seem so terrified this time.

The horse had been captured once and turned lose unharmed. The experience hadn't been a pleasant one for it, but it had no memory of harm either. This time the stud wouldn't be so firmly set on escape. This time it would act almost as a judas goat.

Leon rode loose on the roan. Because Manuela needed

the saddle he was making his rides bareback. That was no problem. The horses, wild so recently themselves, weren't asked for much in the way of speed. All they needed to do was lope along behind the wild ones and keep the bunch moving.

It pleased Leon, though, to realize how well his ribs had healed. He'd been a little worried about that, but the pain now was no more than an annoyance.

The wild herd swept past the coulee where his fences had been reconstructed. The stallion looked like it already was willing to drop off and go to water, but a scruffy-looking mare with gray speckles in a red coat kept going. That one would be the new lead mare, Leon knew. If she turned out to be half as good as the old bitch mare, he would be happy with her.

There weren't as many in this bunch as in the first, but he should get a handful of mares to keep out of them and seven or eight geldings.

Seven or eight geldings would mean more than a hundred dollars when he sold them in Douglas.

He was smiling when he pulled aside and angled toward the camp Manuela had set up.

The mare was saddled and ready. Manuela must have seen the horses pass and knew he would be in in minutes.

"Ready?" he asked as he came near.

Manuela grinned and swung onto the bitch mare.

She mounted more easily now, Leon saw. She knew what she was doing much better than she had that first time. It helped, too, that he had adjusted the stirrup leathers so she could ride properly.

"See you later," she called over her shoulder as she put her heels to the bitch mare and jumped into a run to catch up with the wild ones.

Leon chuckled. He pulled the roan to a halt and slid off its back.

Manuela had left coffee for him hot on a bed of rocks beside the firepit, and there was a pile of freshly made corn cakes on a tin plate.

Yeah, he thought, this was better.

He tended to the roan first, hobbling and brushing it

and checking its feet. Being able to run the wild ones in relays was fairly easy on the horses too. He'd let it cool off before he took it over to the seep for water.

Feeling contented, Leon squatted by the remains of the breakfast fire and helped himself to the coffee and corn cakes. He was already wondering just how much the geldings would bring in Douglas once he had them cut and broken.

Lordy, but it felt good to be out and working again.

33

Leon stopped what he was doing and tied off the rope. It wouldn't hurt the colt to stand tied at the snubbing post for a while. It would be good for him. He pulled his gloves off and walked over to the fence.

"Need some help?"

Manuela shook her head and began unsaddling the old bitch mare. The woman was becoming quite proud of her horsemanship lately.

"Was there any mail?"

"You should not work on the Sabbath," she told him, tugging at the latigo.

He supposed that was an answer of sorts. His disappointment was acute, but there was nothing to be done about it. He was really becoming worried, though.

Manuela slid the saddle off the tall mare, shifted it onto her shoulder, and carried it to the corral, where she had to try twice to heave it onto the top rail. The mare stood ground-tied and patient until Manuela came back and led it inside the enclosure.

"I bought some corn. Fresh. You want it for supper tonight?"

"Sure," Leon said. "I didn't know there were any farmers around here."

"Mexican," Manuela explained. "I shop there, mmm? It is . . . more comfortable." She blinked and for a moment acted like she half-expected him to get mad. "You don' mind?"

"I don't mind."

"Good." She stripped the bridle over the mare's head

and gave the beast an affectionate pat. "Cheaper. Much cheaper."

"Did you get yourself some new clothes?"

"I forgot."

Leon knew damned good and well it was a lie. Manuela simply wouldn't spend anything on herself no matter how hard he insisted.

Probably the only way around it would be for him to go into town himself and buy something for her. She wouldn't take any cash from him. She was certainly entitled to something for all her kindness.

"We go south soon?" She was standing by the breaking-pen fence, peering over the top at the young colt—which soon would be a young gelding—that Leon had been working with this morning.

Somehow, without Leon precisely knowing how it had come about, Manuela had established that she would be going along with him to help drive the geldings to Douglas when Leon decided he was ready to market them.

"Soon," he said.

There would be nine head to take to Douglas. Eight geldings and a mare that was too narrow in the chest to be worth keeping and breeding.

Nine head. That could be near two hundred dollars.

Somehow, dammit, he was going to have to make Manuela accept a share of the profit. She certainly had worked hard enough to help him earn it. It wouldn't be fair to let her go away empty-handed now.

A smile came to him as he decided that, once they were both in Douglas, he could buy something nice for her.

He glanced over toward her.

Definitely a new blouse. Maybe one that buttoned all the way to the throat.

Wouldn't that be a relief.

He was losing entirely too much sleep at night the way things were.

"You ready for lunch, Señor Brown?"

"Yes, thank you."

Manuela stopped at the corral rails long enough to give

the old bitch mare a scratching under the chin, then hurried inside to begin preparing a meal.

Leon pulled his gloves back on and returned to the colt. The youngster rolled its eyes and squealed a protest when it saw him coming. It was going to be a good one, though. Somebody in Douglas was going to get a good mount out of this one.

He spoke softly to the colt. When he picked up the rags he was using to sack the animal out with, he was whistling.

Leon was feeling damn well-contented these days.

34

Leon felt a cold knot form in the pit of his stomach. He looked down in disbelief, then stood in his stirrups and uselessly scanned the horizon.

This had been done days ago. That was obvious at a glance. Yet he couldn't help himself. He felt more frustration than anger and couldn't avoid looking to see if he could spot whoever did this.

"Señor Brown?" Manuela reined closer to him, leaving the small horse herd to stop and begin picking at the scant forage underfoot. "Is something wrong?"

Mutely—he didn't trust himself to speak at the moment—Leon pointed down into the gully.

Manuela had to shift the old bitch mare closer to the edge before she could see.

A heifer lay there, several days dead and bloated. Its calf lay close beside it. Both had been there long enough for coyotes and birds to have been feasting on the carcasses.

"They fell down?" Manuela asked.

Leon shook his head. "They were shot. Some son of a bitch shot them. See?"

"No."

"I . . . Never mind."

"Whose?"

"Mine." The word came out in a croak.

The heifer bore the 3H brand. The calf was too young to be wearing a brand.

"Oh." Manuela stared down into the gully with pity on her homely features. Pity for the calf and cow. Probably pity for Leon as well.

Some son of a bitch—Leon had a good idea who it must have been—had shot down two head of Leon's small herd.

The fact that he, or they, hadn't even taken the un-branded calf, just shot it down and left it to rot in the sun, showed an ugly contempt. They despised him so much that they didn't even want to steal from him. They only wanted to destroy him and probably to hurt him as much as was possible while they did so.

Leon thought about the Colt that rode at his waist and the old Springfield that was slung under Manuela's leg.

He should . . .

It really didn't matter what he should do. The plain fact was that there was practically nothing that he could do. He would be able to prove nothing. Nothing at all. And no amount of guesswork or supposition would carry any weight in a town like Kazumal.

"Let's go," he said.

"But, Señor Brown—"

"Let's go, I said."

Almost savagely he wrenched the roan's head around and pointed it away from the gully and the dead beefs, back toward the horses they were taking to Douglas.

He regretted the impulse as quickly as he'd done it. The fault wasn't the roan's, nor was it Manuela's. He had no call to take out his frustrations by snapping at them.

The fault lay with all the men in Kazumal who hated him because his skin was dark.

The good mood he'd been in this morning was gone now. He wondered if that feeling would ever come back.

35

The drive down to Douglas was a morose and mostly silent affair for Leon, despite Manuela's continual excitement over seeing new country.

Virtually all of Leon's adult life had been spent in motion, shifting here and there at the whim and the need of the cavalry. He found it amazing that Manuela had never been more than twenty-five or thirty miles from Kazumal. And that had been with him when they were on the wild-horse run.

The woman—he didn't want to come right out and ask her age, but after this much association with her, he was guessing it to be somewhere in her early thirties—had never before in her miserable life ventured any farther from the town of her birth than she could walk in a single afternoon. Never.

Now, on horseback and taking a small herd of horses to Douglas, she was vibrant with the pleasure of riding across new land.

Not that there was so much to see between Kazumal and Douglas, of course. Sand and scrub and rock, just like what was around Kazumal. Still, it was sand and scrub and rock that she'd never seen before. And at the end of the drive there would be the sight of a city much larger than Kazumal, a city with bright lights and many stores and even, wonder of wonders, a railroad. Manuela had never seen a railroad before. She barely knew enough about one to know what it was and asked Leon countless questions about rails and engines and the huge cars in which people could ride.

Leon tried to bring back to mind his own first excitement when the army took him far from home and showed him new country and new things.

If his mood had been different, if it were not for the depressing fact that someone was shooting his pitifully few cattle, Leon might very well have entered into Manuela's excitement with her. As it was, he answered her questions with minimal interest and as briefly as possible.

Perhaps the oddest thing about her questioning chatter was that she kept it up even in the face of Leon's reluctance to be drawn into her spirit of adventure.

It didn't occur to him until the last night before they reached Douglas that perhaps Manuela was deliberately pestering him. Perhaps she was trying to draw him out of himself and create a forward-looking mood for him.

That was exactly the sort of thing this kind, thoughtful, pitiful woman would do, he realized after the weeks of care she had given him. The knowledge—if knowledge it was—was almost enough to perk him up from simple gratitude and accomplish her goal.

The last morning, at least, he was able to smile in response to Manuela's squeal of pleasure when they finally came in sight of Douglas and the bright-gleaming steel of the railroad tracks.

Leon allowed her to watch a short freight pull into the Douglas depot as they drove the horses nearer, and she giggled and squirmed in her saddle when the engine blew steam and smoke.

"Oh, Señor Brown, never did I think to see such a sight. Never." She laughed aloud and literally trembled with eagerness to get closer so she could see everything there was to see in the grand city of Douglas.

Leon smiled at her. "Soon as we sell these horses, Manuela, you'll be able to go up and down those streets and shop in every one of those stores. The shipping pens are right on the tracks, you know. You can walk right up to one of those engines and look it over. Why, maybe you can look inside one of the passenger cars and see how the wh—how the rich folks travel."

He didn't want to mention it to Manuela—it might only have served to lessen her excitement—but Leon had never actually seen the inside of a passenger car either. Negroes were allowed passage in baggage or cattle cars, not in passenger coaches. Troopers of the Tenth traveled with their horses and equipment in livestock cars when they moved by rail. Only the officers had been given the privilege of coach travel.

"This is so wonderful," Manuela exclaimed.

Leon smiled again and jogged their small herd into a trot to approach the magic of Douglas.

He stopped a mile out.

"We need to leave the horses here while I figure out what to do with them next," he said.

"I stay with them," Manuela volunteered quickly.

"Thanks."

She shook her head admiringly. "You always know what to do, Señor Brown."

Leon almost laughed at that one. For the past day and a half the fact that he did not know what to do next had been preying on him.

When he was here before, Jud Ramsey had taken care of all the details while Leon stayed back with the cattle and horses that were to be sold.

Ramsey had arranged for the use of pens, found the buyer, and struck the bargain for cattle and horses alike. Now Leon was on his own, and he was frankly unsure how to go about the final steps of marketing his horses.

"I won't be long," he said, hoping he was telling the truth.

Manuela smiled and nodded and leaned down to caress the neck of the ugly old bitch mare that she had begun to call affectionately Chica.

Leon took a deep breath and bumped his roan toward Douglas.

36

The man they directed him to wasn't overtly hostile. Not exactly. But Leon could see the slight pursing of his lips and the tensing of his shoulders when he was approached by a big, heavily muscled black man.

The white man said nothing, but he became instantly wary.

Leon could handle that without conscious thought. He removed his hat and held it before him in both hands, head bobbing slightly and an expression of sheer innocence on his face.

"They tell me you're the man I should see about pennin' some stock." He allowed a slight hint of drawl to enter his speech and deliberately shuffled his right boot in the dirt underfoot.

The station master's scowl lessened, and some of the tension in his body eased as well.

"That's right, boy. Where's your bossman?"

"Jus' a few head o' horses," Leon said. "I'm t' handle 'em by myself." It would only put this man on the defensive again if Leon tried to explain the truth. Better to let it go and let this offay think whatever he pleased.

The station master grunted. "A few head of horses, you say?"

"That's right, mister." Leon knew it would ease things even more if he fell into a "yowzuh, masta" line of bullshit. He wasn't going to do it, though. He was done saying "sir."

The white man motioned for Leon to follow and set off at a fast pace toward the pens without looking back. He stopped finally and pointed. "You can use that pen in the corner there if it's big enough. Fifteen cents per head per day. That includes water in the trough there. If they're here long enough to need feed, you buy that and feed 'em yourself.''

"Fifteen cent a head a day," Leon repeated as if trying to memorize it so he could repeat it for his nonexistent bossman.

"You want me t' write that down for you, boy?''

"No, I got it now, thank you.'' Leon realized the station master probably thought he was being considerate and accommodating. He really didn't intend the offer to be patronizing. Although it was. "Thank you,'' Leon said again.

The station master nodded. "You want the pen?''

Leon started to bob his head and twist his hat brim in his big hands. But, dammit, that was patronizing too, he realized. He quit the habitual playacting and stood upright and proud. "I want the pen, thank you.''

The man looked at him for a moment, then turned and bawled, "Joey! This boy here's gonna bring some horses in t' number eight. You come work the gate, hear?''

"Be right there, boss.'' There was nothing at all subservient about Joey's use of the word "boss'' to the man who was indeed his boss. Leon noticed the difference and idly wondered about it.

He thanked the station master again and turned back toward the roan. "I'll have 'em up in just a bit. Left them a mile out.''

"Joey will take care of it. See me about the rent when you get them in. I'll be in the office this end of the depot. Right?''

"Right.''

Fifteen cents per head per day. Leon wondered why Jud Ramsey hadn't ever mentioned that to him when they were here before.

He didn't want any damned . . .

Then he smiled to himself as he rode back toward Manuela and the waiting horses. There was such a thing as being too sensitive, he supposed. The rent thing had been a kindness on Ramsey's part, not a charity.

He urged the roan into a lope.

37

Leon stepped hesitantly into the hotel lobby, hat in hand and acting meek. This time it wasn't playacting. He'd never in his life been inside so grand a structure, and he felt overwhelmed by the splendor of it. The woodwork and ceilings were ornately carved, and the chandeliers were like something out of a painting rather than real life. Even the wallpaper was fuzzy with some velvety textured stuff in a fancy pattern.

A man behind the counter saw him and hurried out toward him, becoming flushed with rising anger as he came closer. "Here now, what do you think you're—"

"I . . . I'm looking for a Mr. Evans. Livestock buyer from, uh, New Orleans. I thought he might, uh, be here."

The clerk stopped and gave Leon a look of dark suspicion. "Mr. Evans, you say?"

Leon nodded. He rolled his eyes apprehensively around the room, taking in the frighteningly plush surroundings. Why, on furniture that grand a man wouldn't hardly feel comfortable sitting. He would all the time be worrying that he might have something on the seat of his pants that would soil the upholstery. Leon had the vague suspicion that there would be hell to pay if anyone dirtied anything this nice.

His discomfort somehow seemed to soothe the belligerence of the hotel clerk. The man grunted. "If Evans sent for you, I suppose—"

"William. Wait a moment." Another man walked up, a man with a large belly and a suit tailored to minimize it. "Did I hear Nelson Evans mentioned? Is that who you're looking for, young man?"

The newcomer was in his fifties or so, certainly old enough to call someone Leon's age "young." But the fact that he did so—instead of calling him "boy" or "nigger" or something of that ilk—was amazing.

Even more, he held his hand out in an offer to shake. "I'm Jake Hitchins," he said. "And I'd like to have a word with you before William here goes to look for Evans."

Flabbergasted, Leon blinked and allowed this Hitchins to shake with him. Hitchins, though. Where had he heard that name before? Leon felt fairly sure that he had, but he couldn't place whatever context it might have been in.

"Unless my memory's failed me, you would be, no, don't tell me, it'll come to me in a moment." Hitchins' brow knitted in concentration, then he smiled. "Brown. Of course. Mr. Brown of Kazumal. That is correct, is it not?" He was beaming with pleasure at his own powers of recall.

"Why . . . yeah. How'd you know that?"

Hitchins laughed and took him by the elbow, guiding him out of the lobby and onto the broad porch of the hotel. He practically placed Leon in one of the rocking chairs put there for the comfort of the hotel guests and drew another chair close to it.

"Pardon me if I don't offer you a drink, Mr. Brown, but I don't think—"

"No, I reckon that wouldn't be such a good idea, Mr. Hitchins. But I thank you for thinking of it."

Leon was thoroughly confused. What in hell was this man Hitchins being so nice for?

"I daresay you're probably wondering what this is all about, eh, Mr. Brown?"

Leon nodded mutely.

"Simple," Hitchins declared, beaming still. "I happen to be familiar with the consignment of horses Evans bought from you earlier this year, Mr. Brown." He brought out a pair of cigars and offered one to Leon. When Leon declined, he replaced one inside his coat and used a silver cutter to nip the tip from his own selection.

"Fair-quality horseflesh, Mr. Brown. You obviously know that yourself."

Leon nodded uncertainly.

"But tip-top training, sir."

Hitchins seemed to think nothing of it, but no white man had ever come remotely close to calling Leon something like that before.

"I was impressed by those animals, Mr. Brown. Each of them had a first-class handle on them. Good rein, good stop, and no bad habits that I ever heard of. And believe me, I would have heard." Hitchins grinned and puffed on his stogie.

"That damned Evans just lucked into them, of course. But those horses are just the ticket for a man who spends serious time in a saddle. Now the thing is this, Mr. Brown. Evans is primarily a cattle buyer who also deals now and then in horses. I, on the other hand, am primarily a horse buyer who now and then turns a dollar on a cow. I represent a firm dealing at the horse market in San Antonio. You've heard of the market there?"

Leon nodded. Everyone had likely heard about the San Antone market. It was the biggest in the whole country when it came to horseflesh.

"Now, the thing is, Mr. Brown, Evans gave you a fair price for the quality of breeding in those horses you sold him. But a bargain price for horses trained as well as those geldings were." Hitchins grinned and nodded, as if he thought he had just explained the whole thing.

As far as Leon was concerned, he surely had not.

"You understand, of course, that I am making an assumption here. I mean, I recognize you from the last time you were in Douglas. You are, um, noticeable, shall I say?" He laughed, no sting at all in the reference to Leon's color. "And I am assuming—no, hoping—that you are here to market more of those beautifully trained animals. Is that correct, Mr. Brown?"

Leon found himself nodding again. The stout man was more than a little overwhelming in his enthusiasm for his subject. Damned well flattering too.

"The thing is, Mr. Brown—and I must admit that I

feel somewhat guilty also as a result of that unfortunate affair with the, um, Tucker boys—''

That was where Leon had heard the man's name before. He was the man who had unknowingly bought Leon's stolen cattle from the Tuckers.

''—but that really has nothing to do with the proposition I wish to make now.''

Maybe they were finally getting down to the meat of this matter, Leon hoped.

''What I want to do, Mr. Brown, is buy your horses.'' Hitchins beamed again. ''I can get top dollar for them in San Antonio. I don't mind telling you that. I intend to make a fair profit on them for myself. And frankly, Mr. Brown, I would like to assure myself of a future supply from any horses you wish to train and sell.'' He puffed happily on his cigar. ''Are you with me, Mr. Brown?''

''I . . . I'm not sure. Mr. Evans paid me twenty-two—''

''Twenty-seven fifty, Mr. Brown,'' Hitchins said quickly.

Leon blinked. He didn't know what to say. That much money was . . .

Hitchins laughed. ''I see you've done business before, Mr. Brown. Never take the first offer, eh? All right. Twenty-eight fifty. But I can't go a penny higher. Is that acceptable? And at that price you have to promise you'll come to me first the next time you have horses to sell. Is that fair, Mr. Brown?''

Leon blinked.

Hitchins was grinning. He was extending his hand to shake again and seal the deal. Why . . .

Leon reached out and shook Jake Hitchins' pudgy hand, and the stout man laughed.

''Done, Mr. Brown. Done and done. And believe me, sir, it should turn out to be a profitable arrangement for both of us.''

''I have, uh, just nine head this time. Eight geldings and a mare.''

''The mare works as well as the geldings?''

"Yes. Sure." Leon was still in something of a daze from all this.

"Then the deal stands, Mr. Brown. Twenty-eight fifty per head. And I'll expect to see you again whenever you're ready. The horses are at the railyard?"

Leon nodded mutely.

"Excellent. Excellent." Hitchins rubbed his hands together, and Leon guessed the fellow was going to make a nice profit indeed on a bunch of horses Leon really had thought next to worthless.

Not that Leon minded Hutchins making a profit on the horses. Leon certainly had no use for them. And, damn, he knew horses. Here he had come out to Arizona thinking to raise cattle and knowing nothing about cattle. But horses. Now that was something he did know more than a little about. And he had those mares back on the place, and . . .

He began to grin just as broadly as Jake Hitchins was.

Wait until Manuela heard this.

He blinked again. That really wasn't right. Wait until Anne May learned this. She was going to be so proud.

Leon felt his chest swell. He sat back in the rocking chair and heard with only half an ear while Hitchins talked about meeting after dinner to sign over the bills of sale and collect his money for the nine head of horses he had just sold to this odd, ebullient fat man.

Why, things were looking up again despite the Tucker family and those dead cattle back home. Leon was going to have to do something to celebrate this wonderful turn of events.

38

Leon's euphoria lasted through that afternoon and on into the night.

He might not be welcome as a guest anywhere, but the merchants of Douglas or any other town would always be willing to take his money.

Leon treated himself to a new shirt and a fine new razor and strop to replace the old shaving gear he'd owned since his first weeks in the army.

For Manuela he bought two blouses and a red skirt. Her old things were little better than rags. And neither of these new blouses would gap at the throat when she bent forward, thank goodness. It was becoming more and more uncomfortable for him to have to deny his impulses whenever her breasts were inadvertently displayed.

Manuela tried to make him take the things back when he gave them to her, but she was crying when she said it and he was sure the tears contained pleasure rather than pain. It was entirely possible that no one had ever given her a gift before. Leon insisted that she change into her new clothes, and at their camp that night she paraded continually back and forth in what she obviously considered to be entirely grand finery. That response alone was enough to make the purchases worthwhile.

While he was in town, he resupplied too with coffee and cornmeal and enough fresh beef for several meals. The beef was a considerable treat after the game they had both been eating for the past several months.

"You seem happy, Señor Brown," Manuela said after supper.

He smiled. "I think I am, at that."

"Good." She leaned forward, and he was doubly thankful that she was wearing the new blouse. Without asking she gave him the last of the coffee.

"Thanks." The tin can he was using for a cup was too hot to hold. He set it down. "You've been a big help to me, Manuela. More than just a help, really. I don't know how to repay you for all you've done, but—"

"Señor Brown. Please, no. It was only a thing I could do. You owe me nothing."

"I insist, Manuela. I'm not what you'd call experienced at hiring, so I don't know what would be exactly fair. But you know I got a lot more than I expected for those horses. It'd only be right for me to pay you something." He took a pair of double eagles from his pocket, proceeds from the sale to Jake Hitchins, and pressed them into her hand.

Manuela's eyes went wide. "Señor Brown!" Her voice was tight. "No. I could not."

"Please." He meant it. It would please him to be able to repay her kindness, if only with money.

"I could not."

He smiled. "You must."

She tried to argue with him, but Leon's mind was set on the subject and he wouldn't listen to her refusals. He'd given it thought during the afternoon and was determined now to make her take the pay.

Eventually Manuela gave in. But for some reason she seemed sad after she did.

Soon she left the dying fire and went to make out a pallet of blankets on the ground.

"Good night, Señor Brown."

"Good night, Manuela."

This time, with none of the Tucker family in town, no one disturbed Leon's camp during the night.

39

They stopped at the *tinaja*—the one Leon walled off when chasing the wild horses, but the temporary walls had been removed now, of course—and watered the sturdy roan and Chica, the old bitch mare that had more or less become Manuela's.

"Is not far now?" Manuela asked.

Leon smiled. "A couple hours and we'll be home."

It occurred to him that Manuela likely would be wanting to move on now. He no longer really needed her help—although in truth he had come to enjoy her company—and she had some money of her own now. Enough that she could go to another town if she wished. Start fresh somewhere where there would be no burden of Apache blood placed against her. He wondered if he should suggest it to her.

Whatever happened, he decided, he would give her the old bitch mare. Chica, he corrected himself. He was going to have to start thinking about the mare as Manuela's Chica and not just as the old bitch. That would mean giving her the saddle too, of course. But that would be all right. He could find another. Not at the livery in Kazumal but somewhere.

He was going to miss Manuela. He really was.

It would be better for her to leave, though. Anne May would be here soon, and there would be no place for Manuela on the 3H once Anne May arrived. Leon might not know very much about women, but he certainly knew that much: no two of them could live under one roof even if there wasn't a difference in color to set their teeth to grinding.

Funny, he thought, how Manuela didn't seem to worry about that. Funny nice, that is. He . . .

He pulled the roan to a halt and reached over to grab Chica's reins before Manuela rounded the spire of pale rock they were nearing.

"What . . . ?"

"Shhh!"

Leon slid off the roan's back and tossed Manuela his reins. "Stay there."

"Señor Brown?" She sounded frightened, probably from his sudden change of expression, but he had no time right now to comfort her.

"Stay where you are, dammit."

She nodded, but he didn't see. He was bent low to the ground and was scuttling forward in a crablike approach to the point of rock.

Leon dropped to his belly, ignoring the sharp stab of stones and hair-thin cactus spines. He wriggled forward to the side of the rock protrusion and removed his hat before peering cautiously out onto the open ground to the north.

"Damn," he muttered.

"What is it, Señor Brown?" She had sense enough, at least, to whisper.

Leon shook his head and crawled back away from the rock. When he judged it safe, he stood and hurried back beside Manuela, still seated nervously on Chica.

"Apache," he said in a low, calm tone. "I saw the dust. They're not but a hundred fifty yards or so ahead and moving west."

Sudden fear slackened Manuela's features, and she went pale beneath the warm brown of her skin. A hand leapt involuntarily toward her throat.

"We must've been at the *tinaja* when they came up over the rise, or they'd've seen us sure. We're lucky they didn't stop to water too."

He was thinking while he talked. The talk was mostly just to reassure Manuela.

It was a raiding party. He'd seen enough of them to know. And a large one. There must be two dozen riders in the group, and as far as he could tell, there weren't more than two or three women with them. On the plains back East a party with women along meant hunters. Not so with the Apache.

Leon couldn't remember hearing about a broncho bunch in years, though, with more than eight or ten warriors in it. Three or four was more like it these days for the most part. But not this crowd. And if he had actually seen so many, there was no telling how many others were with them that he hadn't seen.

He looked off toward the northeast, wondering if there were any stragglers that might spot Manuela and him. He saw nothing, nor was any dust rising in that quarter.

"It's going to be all right," Leon said. Manuela was trembling. He reached up and patted her hand.

He went forward again and looked around the spire that had saved them from discovery.

The Apache had stopped. A number of them were gathered close together, talking and gesturing toward the northwest.

Kazumal lay pretty much due north. And anyway no group of Apache was likely to attack a whole town. Even if there was a general breakout from one of the reservations, they wouldn't be foolish enough to take on a town. Not this side of the border, anyway, where so many civilians went armed.

Leon's own 3H Ranch was nearly on a line between the *tinaja* and Kazumal, so the Indians were not heading for it. And Jud Ramsey's place lay even farther to the east than the 3H.

It was obvious the Apache had some particular destination in mind, and the only thing Leon could think of that lay ahead of them would be the Tucker ranch.

For an instant he felt a hot, vicious surge of serves-them-right.

But it didn't.

No one, no one, deserved that.

Leon had seen the work of Apache renegades before. He'd buried strangers and he'd buried friends after them. When there was enough left to bury. He shuddered, thinking about it. Apaches were ugly-acting sons of bitches, and no man deserved an end at their hands. No woman either. There probably were women at the Tucker place.

He stood for a moment watching until the raiders drifted apart and once again set out at a leisurely pace toward the northwest, following the contours of the ground and acting like they had all the time in the world to accomplish their filth.

Leon grunted softly to himself. Unconsciously he fingered the butt of the Colt on his hip. When he did that, he heard a sharp intake of breath from Manuela behind him.

"It's all right," he said quickly. He turned and hurried back to her. He took the roan's reins from her shaky fingers and smiled. "It's going to be all right. Really. Here's what I want you to do . . ."

40

Leon watched with some apprehension until Chica was down into the wash and moving east.

He felt better when he knew Manuela was safely away, headed first for Jud Ramsey's place and then, together with Ramsey, on a fast run for Kazumal.

She had the Springfield slung on her saddle. She knew how to use it. Hopefully it wouldn't come to that.

Leon sat bareback on the roan for a moment, although there was no time to waste. He tugged the brim of his hat low over his eyes and bumped the roan into motion. A trot at first so little dust would rise. Then, as soon as he passed behind the long ridge that would shield him from the by-now-distant Apache, into a hard run.

The roan was already warm from the morning's travel, but it wasn't tired. Through his thighs and calves Leon could feel the muscles of the horse moving smoothly and well as he rode north beside the ridge.

Cactus and rock and greasewood flowed under the horse's belly, Leon riding balanced and light over the withers. Speed was needed. But not so much that the roan would play out before he got there.

This was something Leon had done before.

As a corporal he sometimes led patrols. But as a private he had frequently been called on to ride through hostile country alone, acting as a courier for Capt. Carroll or Lt. Thomas.

He rode head high, alert for ambush, Colt holstered but ready if he had to use it.

They cleared the north end of the long ridge and Leon

swung the roan in a gentle turn to the west, lining directly for the Tucker ranch now.

Ramsey had told him where the Tucker place lay. He took a sight on a distant hump of low, barren mountain and guided the roan just north of it. The Tucker ranch was in a valley somewhere between the 3H and that mountain. If he cut the road between the Tuckers and Kazumal, he had gone too far north. If he missed the valley and rode south of the ranch . . . He decided not to think about that possibility. If he did that, there would be only dead Tuckers and live Indians between him and safety.

The Apaches were moving slowly and enjoying their anticipation of the raid.

He should have time. Just.

Fifteen miles lay between the ridge and the Tucker spread. But the roan's gait was fluid and loose, and the horse was strong, accustomed to the miserable pickings of desert graze but well-fed throughout the summer.

Leon eased back on the bit a little, allowing the horse to collect itself and do its work.

On a long run make haste slowly. That was what Lt. Thomas always told them.

Leon raised his chin and let the hot breeze of the run flow over him.

Sons of bitches or not, he wasn't going to allow the Tuckers or anyone else to be taken by surprise. He had to warn them.

The roan was sweating but not heavily lathered. The horse was a good one. Leon reined it to a walk and let it pick its way down the bank to the flat, sloping floor of the slight depression that Ramsey had termed a valley.

Off to the north not more than three-quarters of a mile Leon could see a scattering of buildings and corrals set in the protection of a grove of cottonwoods.

There was no sign of the Apache. The only smoke was a thin, pale plume rising from the stone chimney of the rambling adobe house. The Tucker women would be preparing the midday dinner. Leon hoped the men came in for lunch. Otherwise he'd have to collect the women and make a run for town with them.

The roan reached level ground again, and he eased it into a fast lope, pleased with the amount of response it had left to give him. Some of the cavalry mounts he had ridden, particularly the near-useless ones issued to the Negro units in the early days, would have been wind-blown and down by now. The roan was better than he had given it credit for.

Off to the south Leon thought he could see a faint, dusty haze hanging in the air.

He had gotten to the Tuckers ahead of the Indian raiders. But not by much.

He rode into the yard at a high lope and slid the roan to a halt.

"Hello the house. Hello."

Without waiting to be asked Leon jumped off the sweaty roan's back and started toward the open doorway.

A woman appeared there, gasped when she saw him, and quickly withdrew. A moment later she was replaced in the doorframe by the bulk of a tall, gray-haired man with a bulging belly and a Spencer carbine.

"What are you doing here, nigger?"

"Apache," Leon spat. "There's a raiding party. Heading this way. They aren't a mile off by now. Maybe less. I saw them. Rode to warn you. You—"

"Get off my property, nigger." The old man—he almost had to be the patriarch of the Tucker clan—raised the Spencer, waving the muzzle in the general direction of Leon's chest.

"But I just told you . . ." Leon was out of breath, even though it was the roan that had just done all the work. "There's Apache coming. I come . . . came . . . to warn you. We got to fort up. Protect your people here."

"Apache, huh?"

"Yeah, dammit. At least two dozen of them. I counted that many. There's probably more. We got to get your people in and fort up." Leon looked quickly around the place. "The house here. You built it for defense. And we can put some men in that adobe-walled pen there. Set up a crossfire from—''

''Don't tell me what t' do, you black-assed son of a bitch.''

Leon stopped and stared incredulously at Tucker. ''I'm trying to tell you—''

''All right. You told me.'' Tucker turned his head so he was facing into the house and bellowed. ''Tom, Corey, break out the rifles. Mother, ring the bell. We got to fort up now. 'Paches comin'.'' He turned back to glare at Leon. ''Satisfied?''

''I . . . suppose so, but—''

''Now get out.'' He waved the menacing barrel of the carbine again.

''What!''

''Get off my property, nigger. Right now. We don't want your kind.''

Leon couldn't believe what he was hearing. They wanted him to ride out? Now? With Apache raiders only minutes away, perhaps by now circling to the north too?

It was . . . unthinkable.

Old Man Tucker obviously didn't think so. He motioned Leon away again with the muzzle of the Spencer. ''Get out.''

''You're actually sending me away? After I've come here to warn you people?''

''Get out. Now.''

Leon glanced over his shoulder toward the south.

There was no dust now. No sign at all of the raiding party he knew was there. That meant the Indians were already split up and closing in on the place.

Not seeing Apaches when you knew they were near was worse than seeing them.

''Are you gonna git, or am I gonna save them Apache the trouble of lifting your kinky hair?''

Tucker had been joined now by two young men, also armed, who looked entirely ready to start it with Leon if their father didn't want to bother. Leon recognized both of them. They had both participated in his beating at the smithy.

"Jesus," Leon said.

Tucker raised the Spencer again and eased the hammer back to full cock.

Leon turned and swung lightly onto the roan's back. The sweat that soaked the seat of his trousers bunched the wet cloth and made it pinch and sting. That, however, wasn't the worst of his worries at the moment.

"Git!" one of the boys shouted.

Leon didn't bother looking to see which one of them it was. It hardly seemed to matter right now.

He paused just long enough to give the Tuckers a hard glare.

Then he pointed the roan north toward Kazumal and put it into a trot.

The question now was whether any of the raiders had already circled around to get between the ranch and the town.

If they had, Leon had a gauntlet to run for his safety.

He leaned forward and stroked the hot, wet neck of the roan. "Let's pick it up, girl."

Behind him a warning bell began to ring, and more Tuckers came dashing out of a shed to see what the alarm was.

Leon didn't look back.

41

The so-called valley had been shallowly cut by a seasonal creek. Leon angled the roan mare into a tangle of dense brush along the now-dry creekbed. If the Apache were ahead of him, they'd be concentrating on the house, where now the bell was wildly clanging and men were shouting.

Or so Leon hoped, anyway.

He pulled the horse down to a slow walk. Stealth was much more important now than speed. His best hope was to get out without being spotted.

He still couldn't believe, though, that Tucker had sent him away to face the Apache alone.

God, but that was hate in its purest form.

The brush Leon was riding through thinned, and he leaned low over the roan's neck to minimize the bulk he was presenting for view.

His heart was beating fast now, and there was a lump in his throat. There was no getting used to the idea that a bullet might come crashing into one without warning.

Leon had done this sort of thing before. It wasn't something he was ever likely to learn to accept.

For a moment, uselessly, he wished he had a squad of the old crowd with him. No one cursed and refused their help. Not when there were hostiles on the move. Those black-assed sons of bitches, as Tucker would call them, had proven themselves.

Well, dammit, so had Leon. More times and in more ways than that old fart likely had.

His expression firmed, and he gentled the roan with a

soft word and a stroke of his palm. The horse was becoming nervous, taking that from its rider, of course.

Leon smiled grimly to himself. The Apache hadn't gotten him before, and neither had the Comanche or the Kiowa or the border thieves. They'd all had their tries. The Apache weren't going to take him this time either.

He rode slowly, ears tuned acutely. He was more likely to hear danger than see it. The twang of a bowstring, the click of a hammer being cocked, the crunch of leaves or gravel under a moccasined foot—those were the things he had to listen for.

He slipped the retaining thong off the hammer of the Colt on his belt. Without that the revolver might be bounced loose if the horse got rowdy or had to run. But the thong made the weapon slower to get into action.

Leon followed the dry creekbed until it curved off to the west toward some larger, unseen watercourse. He left it and eased the mare onto the bank, slipping silently through the brush to bare ground beyond.

A slight rise led to another ridge ahead. The east end of this ridge overlooked the Tuckers' wagon road to Kazumal. If there were any raiders at this end of the valley, that was where they'd be, watching the road and guarding it against escape from the ranch.

Leon grunted softly to himself and directed the roan around the west end of the ridge instead.

As he reached it, he looked back.

He could see the ranch clearly from the slight elevation. Even as he watched, a pair of Indians darted out of the scrub on the valley floor and made for the protection of the stone well in the Tucker yard.

A puff of white smoke appeared from one of the slit windows in the thick adobe wall of the ranch house, followed a moment later by the sound of the report.

The nearer Apache dropped flat. The other one disappeared with ghostlike quickness.

From the house the defenders wouldn't be able to see the first one on the ground, Leon suspected. They probably thought they killed him, but from where Leon watched he could see the Apache make a hand signal to another warrior and crawl backward.

More raiders circled in behind the house, surrounding it now with a ring of carbines.

Anyone who said the Apache were poorly armed was misinformed. At best. This crowd had come to fight, and it looked like they were going to make a siege of it.

Three of them popped into sight on the far side of the adobe pen but were quickly driven back by a volley of gunfire from behind the thick walls of the corral.

So Tucker had taken his advice, Leon thought without satisfaction. Or maybe it was a plan worked out years ago. Leon neither knew nor cared. Whatever, however, the Tuckers would be able to hold out for a while.

Not indefinitely, though. Leon could see more raiders approaching from the south. A separate party? More than the two dozen he had already seen, anyway.

He turned the roan away and rode slowly, quietly behind the ridge.

Leon rounded the boulder and almost rode into the middle of three of them.

The Apache were lying behind a low bank of earth, much farther north than Leon guessed, lying in ambush beside the road to Kazumal.

The roan had been moving silently or they surely would have heard him coming. Or perhaps they'd been talking, their own noise covering the sound of his approach.

Whatever the reason, he was into them before he knew it. Sitting high above them on the back of the roan mare while the Apache lay flat on the ground with their Winchesters aimed away from him. Not twenty feet away from him.

Leon grabbed for his Colt.

One of the Apache heard or saw or somehow sensed the danger. The warrior turned and shouted something.

Leon thumbed the hammer of the .45 and triggered a slug into the Apache's chest. The man fell backward, his Winchester flying.

The damned mare, untrained to gunfire, blew up in a

panic at the sound of the muzzle blast close beside its ear, and Leon went flying.

Leon clung desperately to one rein with his left hand. If he lost the horse now, he was dead.

He hit the ground hard, and the Colt discharged, the bullet slamming into the ground in front of him and ricocheting into the meaty thigh of another warrior.

Both Apache were trying to bring their carbines to bear. They were hampered only by the surprise and by the fact that the long guns were awkward at such close range.

Leon shot one of them.

The other fired, and gravel sprayed into Leon's face, opening small cuts and stinging like hell.

The mare tried to pull away and run, but Leon had the end of the rein wrapped tight around his fist and he held on for his life. The roan pulled him sideways over the gravely soil, spoiling his aim as he tried to shoot the remaining warrior.

The Apache fired first, and Leon felt the heel of his boot jerk with all the power of a blacksmith's hammer.

He waited for the roan to pause in its struggles, took careful aim—the Apache was having trouble levering a fresh cartridge into his Winchester—and shot the man.

Leon jerked the rein and barked sharply at the roan. The horse steadied and Leon came to his knees.

At least one of the Indians was still alive. No, two of them. They were groaning and writhing, though, and out of the mood for a fight right now.

Leon shoved the Colt back into his holster, collected the other rein, and spun the roan for a moment to confuse and settle it so he could jump onto its back.

As soon as he was seated, he jammed his heels into the horse's barrel and jumped it into a hard run on the road to Kazumal.

"Lordy," he yelped as he bent low over the mare's neck and raced for town.

42

The roan was worn out by the time Leon finally nursed it onto the main street of Kazumal. He could feel the animal's muscles tremble and strain between his knees, and it was carrying its head low. The lather that Leon sat in was hot and slimy and stung his skin.

It had made it, though. That was the important thing.

A group of men were gathered outside a saloon. Jud Ramsey was with them. So was Manuela. They seemed to be arguing.

Leon slid off the roan's back and walked it the last fifty yards or so. Now that it sensed the run was over, the roan was staggering and clumsy-footed.

"Here's the nigger now," one of the men in the crowd said.

Hostile looks greeted him. Manuela rushed out to meet him, and Ramsey motioned for Leon to join them.

He gave the roan's reins to Manuela and went to stand beside his neighbor.

"What's this about Apache?" someone demanded. The man wore a badge pinned to his shirt, although Leon couldn't recall ever seeing a lawman in Kazumal before now.

Leon nodded. "Thirty, maybe forty of them. Helluva big raiding party anyway. They've got the Tuckers surrounded. When I left the Apache were still drawing fire. Counting guns, I'd say. Trying to get a look at what they're up against. I'd say they'll like get the Tuckers to burn ammunition all afternoon and then fire the house once it's coming dark."

"That's what you'd say, eh, nigger?"

Leon looked the man in the eyes and calmly told him, "That is what I would say based on fifteen years in the cavalry, yes."

"Hell, there's prob'ly not a 'Pache this side of the San Carlos," another man said loudly. "We haven't heard anything about a breakout."

"You think what you like, mister, but that family isn't going to make it if there isn't a relief party goes out to help them. They're surrounded. And those Apache didn't come to play. I had to fight my way through them to get here."

The livery man—Leon couldn't remember the man's name and didn't want to—sneered. "Got yourself caught, did you? I notice you run out on the white family you're so het up to save now."

Leon removed his hat and wiped sweat from his face. The gravel cuts from that Apache's bullet stung when he disturbed the crusted blood on the gashes. There was no point in trying to explain the truth, so he didn't try.

"The point is," Jud Ramsey cut in, "there's a raid going on. We have to do something about it."

"We only have the nigger's word for that. Hell, even the slut here didn't see the 'Paches herself. She said so. She just took the nigger's word for it too."

Ramsey stopped the man with a cold look. "We're wasting time," he said. "If we don't drive the raiders off from the Tucker place, we'll all have to face them whenever and wherever they choose." He turned to Leon. "You think they're dug in enough that they'll still be there to be caught, Mr. Brown?"

"I do, Mr. Ramsey."

Ramsey turned to face the lawman. "Well, John?"

The marshal or sheriff or whatever he was looked nervous. He cleared his throat before he spoke. Then he turned to face the crowd in general. "Ten minutes," he said. "Saddle up and get your rifles. We'll meet back here in ten minutes."

The only one of the whole bunch willing to so much as look at Leon was Jud Ramsey. Ramsey took him by the elbow. "Thanks," he said. "We owe you." He smiled and winked. "All of us."

Leon nodded and went back to where Manuela was standing with the roan.

"Where's the—I mean, where's Chica?"

Manuela pointed toward the Mexican end of town. "At the rail. Down near the church."

"Thanks." Leon started in that direction.

"Señor Brown."

"Yeah?"

"Be careful?"

He smiled at her. "Thanks."

43

They stopped behind the ridge, not far from the place where Leon had had the unexpected gunfight. There was no sign now of the Apache he had shot, but bloodstains showed where they had been.

The men from Kazumal looked grim, their faces devoid of animation and the sweat heavy on them. There were more than twenty in the group with the lawman named John in charge.

"There's no good cover that I can see and no way to sneak up on them. Once we come around this ridge here, we'll be in view. So I say we just charge like hell and hope for the best." He glanced at Leon, sitting the old bitch mare at the back of the bunch, but didn't ask him anything.

Actually it was probably as good a plan as any. The man was right about there being no cover close enough to do them any good. As late in the afternoon as it was getting, there wouldn't be time for anything fancy even if Leon could think of a better plan. They needed to smash the Indians and send them reeling. From there it would be the army's job to find them and either put them back on the reservation or drive them across the border into the protective wastes of Mexico.

The Apache wouldn't be expecting an attack now. A hard, gun-blazing charge had a good chance of routing them.

Leon kept his mouth shut and eased Chica over to the left so that when the group wheeled to make the charge around the end of the ridge, he would be riding in the fore.

These offay sons of bitches already thought he had run out on the Tuckers once today. He wasn't going to give them the satisfaction of seeing him ride at the back of the pack now.

Of the men only Jud Ramsey noticed what he was doing. Ramsey kneed his horse close to Leon's.

Leon grinned at him. "For a white man you're kinda dumb, Mr. Ramsey. Aren't you getting a little old for this?"

Ramsey grinned back. "For a black man you're getting kinda bold, Mr. Brown. Aren't you supposed to be too cowardly for this?"

Leon chuckled and Ramsey began to laugh. Several of the other men gave them dirty looks.

This time Leon suspected the disapproval had nothing to do with race or color. Those tense, scared civilians were resenting the fact that Ramsey and Leon could find the relief of humor at this moment; that was all.

"All right. Let's go," John said from somewhere in the middle of the crowd.

Leon drew his Colt, the chambers loaded with six rounds now instead of the safe, customary five, and spurred Chica forward to lead the charge around the end of the ridge and down into the valley.

Behind him the others broke into a thundering run, and for a moment it was almost like the old times when the buffalo soldiers were riding at his back.

The brim of Leon's campaign hat was driven down into his eyes by the force of the wind, and he shoved it up so the wind would pin it tight against the battered crown.

He tipped his head back and let out a loud, quavering yell that the men behind him picked up.

An Indian rose up out of nowhere with a Kennedy repeater in his hands. Leon ignored him and raced past. He heard shots behind him and hoped these civilians knew enough to be careful of where they were shooting.

The Tucker ranch yard came closer. Leon continued his wild yelling, and gunsmoke spat from the windows of the adobe house.

A raider spun to face the charge, exposed himself to

the gunfire from the house, and went down with a bullet in the side of his head.

The relief party was still too far away to fire with any effectiveness. Leon leaned low over Chica's neck until the saddle horn gouged him in the stomach. He held his fire and charged closer and closer still.

A group of Apache scattered from behind an over-turned wagon like a bunch of quail taking flight. Leon swerved toward them and bore down on them at a belly-down run.

The renegade Indians were zigging and zagging fran-tically now. Leon chose one, reined Chica slightly so that he was coming up immediately behind the warrior, and shot the man between the shoulder blades.

The gunfire from the rest of the men was slight now. The untrained civilians had expended their ammunition from too far out and many were having to reload so they could shoot some more.

Leon yanked the mare's head around to chase another of the Indians, sent the horse up behind the man, and shot him low in the small of the back.

A third Apache wheeled to face him. A lucky bullet from Leon's Colt smashed into his throat, and the Apache went down.

Off on the other side of the adobe corral Leon could see more of the raiders dart out of cover and begin to run toward the south.

"This way. They've left their horses down this way," he yelled.

Only a few of the civilians seemed interested in follow-ing him. Ramsey was among those that did.

Leon left the rest of the fight to the Tuckers and those who chose to remain in or near the yard, and spurred Chica south.

The Indians had a good lead on his small group. They reached their horses in the creekbed and began mounting.

Leon stopped and peppered them from long range with the last cartridges in the cylinder. The others who had ridden with him stopped where he was and did the same. Leon thought he saw one warrior slump over his horse's back, but at that range they really weren't going to do much good.

Moving from long habit, Leon punched the empties out of the Colt and reloaded it quickly.

"Now sweep back up the creek. There'll be some of them hiding in the brush."

"What about . . . ?"

"Forget them. Believe me, we'll never catch 'em now. Not the ones that've got to their horses."

Leon spurred the mare into the tangle of brush along the creek and began working slowly back toward the grove where the house sat.

Some of the others followed. More broke off and turned back toward the house across open country.

The firing was dying away now. Within minutes there was only an occasional gunshot.

Leon nodded silently to himself. The Apache had gotten a bellyfull this day.

44

Chica seemed almost as tired as Leon was. It had been a hell of a day for both of them.

He rode up to the group of men gathered by the well and dismounted, leading the mare toward a trough one of the men was filling.

"You!"

Leon turned.

"You, nigger. I told you to get off my property." It was the old man. Tucker. He broke off from the others and came toward Leon with his face growing red and his fists knotting. "I threw you out of here before, and I'll do it again, nigger. No black-assed son of a bitch is going to drink out of my well." His lip twisted. "Poison it for all of us, you son of a bitch."

"Mr. Tucker, I am just a little bit tired and out of sorts," Leon said calmly. "I don't think I'm really in the humor for it right now, thank you."

"Get out. Get . . . out!" Tucker was sputtering with rage and looked close to apoplexy.

Leon ignored him and took Chica to the end of the trough. She dipped her muzzle to it, and her ears worked back and forth as if they were pumping the cool, refreshing water into her long throat. Something about that silly motion never ceased to tickle Leon. He just plain liked to watch a horse drink.

"You heard Pa." One of the Tucker boys—Leon couldn't tell them apart even if he wanted to, but he was fairly sure this was one who had been in on the beating that day at the smithy—dashed up and grabbed Leon's shoulder, spinning him half around.

"Get off our land," the boy hissed.

"You surely are an appreciative soul," Jud Ramsey said. "You do realize, don't you, that this man just saved your whole family from being wiped out by those renegades."

"He's a nigger, and we don't want him drinking from our well," the boy snapped.

Ramsey gave the youngster a sad, weary look. "It appears to me, Tommy, that it's Mr. Brown's horse that's drinking your water, not Mr. Brown." He looked at the old man. "Call off your son, Tucker. I think we've all had enough for one day."

The boy, though, wouldn't let it go. He tried to kick the old bitch mare in the muzzle to force here away from the water.

The horse shied momentarily and went back to the trough.

The Tucker boy started to pull a revolver out of his belt.

Leon stepped between him and the mare. "I don't think you want to do that." His eyes narrowed. "Boy!"

Tommy blanched and took a half-step backward. "You nigger son of a bitch."

"Take your hand off that gun, boy, or I swear I'll take it away from you and hurt you with it."

Leon had had enough. E-damn-nough.

The Tucker boy hauled the revolver out.

"Fine!" Leon barked.

He stepped forward. With one hand he plucked the gun out of the boy's fingers and threw it into the well. With the other he backhanded the kid across the face hard enough to snap his head around and bring a yelp out of him. His lip split, and blood began to flow over his chin.

"Why—"

Leon hit him again, low and hard, and turned to take on two more of them who were flying at him from the side.

He battered one face-forward into the ground and lifted the next clean off his feet with a driving blow to the belly.

Another jumped him from behind. Leon rammed the point of his elbow into that one's breadbasket and doubled him over.

He whirled, crouching, ready to take on all the Tucker bastards if he had to.

Ramsey and another man had the old man by the arms and were shouting at him while Tucker shouted encouragement to his sons.

"John!" Ramsey barked.

The Kazumal lawman waded into the middle of it and grabbed one Tucker by the belt and another by the shirt collar. "All right, dammit. That's enough."

"But—"

"Shut up."

The boy shut up.

The lawman looked at Leon. "I'm sorry. Ramsey's right. There isn't any call for this, Brown."

Leon let his fists down and relaxed.

The Tuckers who were picking themselves up gave him dark looks but held their ground. Chica finished drinking, and Leon led her away from the trough a few paces. He didn't drink any of the Tucker water himself. Hell, it would taint the well if he did. He couldn't have that on his conscience.

"Let me tell you something," Jud Ramsey said to the suddenly quiet group of men. "There aren't many of you here who're Catholic. Not that I see at Mass, anyway."

The men looked at him with curiosity. Leon couldn't figure out what that had to do with anything either, though. He couldn't blame them for their confusion.

Ramsey pointed at Leon. "That black man there, the one who's your neighbor now just the same as he's mine, he's put up with enough shit from you people. You ought to be ashamed of yourselves. If you went to Mass you'd've heard Father Felipe using this unwanted outsider as a hell of a lesson for the rest of us. He came here to live calm and quiet, and what's happened to him? He's been cheated. He's been stolen from. He's been beaten. His cows have been shot down by this . . . good citizen here.'' He pointed to Tucker, and all eyes swung onto the old man.

''No, damn you, Matthew, don't you try and deny it. I heard the shots, and I saw Tommy and Nathan finish three head of cows and ride away. Shot down calves too, you have. I've found them. On my range. First you stole Mr. Brown's stock, then you killed what you couldn't steal.''

Tucker's eyes dropped, and he looked like he was squirming, although he didn't try to leave.

This wasn't country where men took lightly the thought of someone stealing or killing livestock on the open range. Not even a black man's livestock. That sort of thing could be a threat to them all if it once got started as a way to escalate grudges. And Leon suspected that Tucker was a man to have grudges with more than just one neighbor.

''Personally,'' Ramsey said, ''I'm fed up with it.'' He looked at the livery man and pointed. ''You tried to cheat him.'' He pointed to another. ''I've heard you talk about tar and feathers, Harry.''

His eyes swept over the crowd. ''You've even gotten pissed off at that poor Manuela because she quit whoring for you for pennies and helped Mr. Brown when some of you beat him half to death. And that poor woman has been walking, walking all the way from Mr. Brown's 3H to town every Saturday night so she could go to Mass like a decent person should. But I don't see any of you in church. Hell, no. That might remind you of what you should be doing. You are your brother's keeper, you stupid sons of bitches.'' Ramsey's eyes flashed. ''Including that one right there who saved a whole bunch of you from dying today.'' He pointed at Leon. ''And led the charge on those Apache, I might add.'' He shook his head. ''Jesus!''

Leon swung into his saddle and began walking the horse away.

''Wait up, Mr. Brown. I'll ride with you.'' It was Ramsey's voice.

Leon pulled the mare to a stop and waited until Ramsey

was mounted and joined him. When they were well out of hearing, he said, "Thank you, Mr. Ramsey. That was a brave thing you did."

Ramsey scowled. "It won't do any good, you know. I won't change their minds about anything any more than the priest can."

"I wouldn't expect you to. Nor him either." Leon looked at his neighbor. They were riding knee to knee. "The priest, that Father Felipe, he really said something about me?"

"Yes."

"And Manuela?"

"You thought she was going to town to whore? So did I. I changed my tune when the father told me she'd been coming to the first-light Mass every Sunday. I expect I owe her an apology. Just like I owe you one."

"You don't owe me nothing, Mr. Ramsey."

"I just wish—"

Leon chuckled. "You figure out a way to change the world, Mr. Ramsey, you let me be the first to know, hear? I'd be satisfied if I could just ride into town without thinking I'm gonna have to defend myself. And probably hang if I do."

Ramsey grunted. "I think I can promise you that much anyway, Mr. Brown. I think we can see to that."

"That'd surely be enough," Leon said with a nod. "Why, that'd be plenty."

Ramsey smiled at him. "Race you to town?"

"Shee-it," Leon said.

Ramsey laughed and kept his horse at a walk.

45

"I hear you've been sticking up for me," Leon said.

Manuela shrugged but didn't answer. They were riding slowly through the moonlight, taking it easy on the exhausted horses.

"Well, I want to thank you. That's all."

Manuela remained silent.

They reached the turnoff and moved onto 3H land. Leon was tired, but he felt a thrill of pleasure to be coming home now to his own place, on his own land.

He felt optimistic too.

He knew better than to think he would be accepted in Kazumal, of course. Even Jud Ramsey admitted that. But it was going to be better now. Not all of the men of Kazumal would hate him. A few of them even seemed to be appreciative. That was a hell of a first step right there. More, in fact, than he could have hoped for.

"That priest," he said.

"Yes?"

"He, uh, seems like a pretty good fella."

"Very good."

"I've never been to a Roman church before. What, uh, do they do there?"

Manuela giggled. "They don' bite heads off babies if tha's what you mean. You want to come with me to Mass?"

"Maybe."

"I take you. Sunday. Very early we go."

"That's another thing," Leon said awkwardly. "I guess I owe you an apology. All this time I've been thinking . . ." He didn't quite know how to finish.

"Is all right. I know what you think. But I only go early to check the mail for you. You know?"

"Damn," Leon said. "I forgot to ask about the mail when I was in town. I don't know how I forgot that. Stupid of me."

Manuela said nothing at all.

They rode on, coming finally in sight of the little ranch house.

"Do you smell something?" Leon asked. He raised his face to the air and sniffed. "Like, I don't know, charcoal?"

"I think—"

"Oh, Lordy," Leon moaned. He booted the roan into a shambling trot.

The walls of the house still stood. But the place had been fired. The roof timbers had burned, and the sod that had been on them was tumbled inside the walls.

The house was ruined. So was practically everything that had been in it.

"Oh, Jesus," Leon said.

He left the roan ground-tied and rushed to what had been his doorway.

Smoldering debris blocked him there.

"No! No, dammit."

Manuela came up beside him and pulled at his elbow, trying to lead him away.

"We will fix it," she said patiently. "The Apache . . . the raiders . . ."

Leon yanked his arm loose from her and tried to get inside. "I have to . . . I have to get it all put back the way it was. Anne May. She'll be here. She might be on her way right now. I have to get it put right again before she sees it like this. You don't . . . you don't know her. She wouldn't . . . wouldn't ever want to live in a mess . . . like this. I got to get it put right again."

Manuela grabbed him and dragged him back.

"But you don't understand. Anne May can't see it like this. I've told her how nice it is, and I can't let her see it like this. She . . . she might walk away and never . . ."
He struggled toward the doorway again.

Manuela got between him and the smoke-stinking remains of the house and pushed against his chest. The top of her head came barely to his chin and she didn't seem particularly strong, but she wouldn't budge to let him by.

"Señor Brown. Please."

Something frantic and unthinking, almost like panic, came over Leon and he tried to bull his way past, but Manuela wouldn't move.

"I have to get it ready for Anne May," Leon insisted blindly. "I have to."

"She is not coming!" Manuela cried. Her homely face twisted with mingled anger and sympathy. "The woman is not coming. Never coming. Please, Señor Brown. Please. Let be. Please?"

Leon stopped trying to reach the house. He blinked and had trouble focusing his thoughts. "What did you say?"

Manuela wouldn't meet his eyes, although she continued to hold on to him to prevent him from trying to get into the house again. "Please, Señor Brown. Please sit. Here. One of those beams, it could fall on you if you go in now. Better to wait for daylight, yes? Please wait."

"But . . . you said something about Anne May?"

Manuela shuddered and kept her head down. "The woman, she is not coming."

"I don't understand. How would you . . . ?"

Very gently she guided him to the front wall and sat him down in the dirt so he could lean back against it. The adobe was warm from the lingering heat of the fire.

"I did not wish to tell you, Señor Brown. Is my fault you were not told. I wanted to keep things . . . as they were. Just a little longer. You know?"

Leon was speechless. He stared into the night and shook his head.

"Señor Ramsey, he wanted to tell you. I said no. I was . . . selfish. Is that the word? I wanted to stay and . . . have things not change."

"I don't understand," Leon said. "What would Mr. Ramsey know about Anne May?"

Manuela looked away from him. "The letter, it came two, three weeks ago. The mail you want. But it was a card thing. You know? Not sealed. At the store, when I pick up the mail, some of the men they are laughing. Saying things. They have read the card with the writing on it. And I didn' want you to be unhappy. So I take it to Señor Ramsey to read. The cards says this woman of yours will not come. It says if you don' have the pay, you know, from army after you leave?''

"Retirement pay." Leon felt numb.

"It says she won' come now and be poor.''

"But—"

"Shhh. I know. I know. Shhh." Manuela laid a fingertip over his lips to hush him. "You are not poor, Señor Brown. An' any woman should be proud to have a man so fine as you. So strong an' good a man as you. This one, pah''—she spat to the side—''she don' deserve you anyhow.'' Manuela tried to hold him, tried to comfort him.

"I don't understand," Leon said.

But he did. He was beginning to.

Anne May wasn't on her way to him. She never would be.

"The postcard. Do you have it?''

"I hide it. Inside. I look for it tomorrow. Maybe it did not burn up.''

Leon craned his neck to stare blindly toward what the Apache had left of his home.

"I suppose it doesn't matter now anyway.'' His voice was dull and lifeless.

"You don' give up, Señor Brown. Why, you have everything here. Good start to raise the horses,' yes? Good place to sell all you raise. We can fix the house. The walls, they will be good. We cut more *vigas*, cut sod. You and me, Señor Brown, we make it right again. We get a good sleep tonight, an' tomorrow we start to fix everything.''

"I don't know if it's worth fixing, Manuela. Not anymore I don't.'' He peered off into the darkness. "A man, even a black man . . . I can't face the idea of living alone all my life, Manuela. I just can't. And there's not any other blacks, I don't know, closer than east Texas, maybe, or Denver or some such. I just can't. . . ."

"Señor Brown?"

He acted like he hadn't heard.

Manuela crept into his lap and laid her face against his broad chest. "Please, Señor Brown. Before you came . . . You made me feel like real person for the first time. Ever. I would stay with you. Work beside you. Give to you what I can. I know I am not your lady. But I would do what I can."

Leon closed his eyes. He could feel tears welling hot under his eyelids.

Manuela moved slightly. Subtly inviting. Gently prompting.

Leon responded. He couldn't help it.

"We are both people without people," Manuela said.

Leon nodded.

He would be an outsider here for the rest of his life. He knew that. So would Manuela.

But this was his land, dammit. He did have a future here. If he wanted to make it so.

Manuela touched him, hesitant and shy but encouraging him if he wished it.

Tomorrow, Leon thought. They could start rebuilding tomorrow.

And maybe, just maybe . . .

Leon groaned and wrapped his arms around the poor, sad, vulnerable, Mexican/Apache outcast.

Just maybe . . .

ABOUT THE AUTHOR

Frank Roderus is the author of *Leaving Kansas*, which won the Western Writers of America's 1983 Spur Award. He is also the author of Signet's *The Ballad of Bryan Drayne*. He currently lives in Colorado Springs, Colorado.